A Pocketful of Stars

Jaap Tuinman

CONSULTANTS

Sharon Anderson

Elaine Baker

Maxine Bone

Jill Hamilton

Diana Hill

Orysia Hull

Sandy Johnstone

Moira Juliebö

Beverley Kula

Helen Langford

Mary Neeley

Carol Pfaff

Sharon Rich

Rosemary Wiltshire

PROGRAM EDITOR

Kathleen Doyle

GINN

Ginn Publishing Canada Inc.

JOURNEYS

A Pocketful of Stars

Anthology Level Seven

EDITORS

Monica Kulling

Jean Stinson

EDITORIAL CONSULTANT

Nicki Scrimger

ART/DESIGN

Sandi Meland Cherun/
Word & Image Design Studio

C99201

ISBN 0-7702-1735-4

Printed and bound in Canada.
CDEFGH 97654321

Acknowledgments

Acknowledgment is hereby made for kind permission to reprint the following material:

My Name Is Not Odessa Yarker, ©1977 by Marian Engel. First published by Kids Can Press, Toronto. Reprinted by permission of the Estate of Marian Engel.

"The Elephant Hunter" by Lorrie McLaughlin. First published in *Nunny Bag 5,* copyright ©1966 W.J. Gage Limited, *Expressways, Teacher's Sourcebook 6,* copyright ©1978 Gage Publishing Limited. Reprinted by permission of Gage Educational Publishing Company.

Text and illustrations for excerpt from *Rosie and Michael* by Judith Viorst, illustrated by Lorna Tomei. Text copyright ©1974 Judith Viorst. Pictures copyright ©1974 Lorna Tomei. Reprinted with permission of Atheneum Publishers, an imprint of Macmillan Publishing Company.

Everybody Needs a Rock, text copyright ©1974 Byrd Baylor. Reprinted by permission of Charles Scribner's Sons, an imprint of Macmillan Publishing Company.

Text and illustrations for *Taking Care of Crumley,* text copyright ©1984 by Ted Staunton, illustrations copyright ©1984 by Tina Holdcroft. Reproduced with permission of the publisher, Kids Can Press Ltd., Toronto.

"The Pain" from *The Pain and The Great One,* copyright ©1974 by Judy Blume. Reprinted with permission of Bradbury Press, an Affiliate of Macmillan, Inc.

Excerpt from *Jacob Two-Two and the Dinosaur,* copyright ©1987 by Mordecai Richler. Used by permission of the Canadian Publishers, McClelland and Stewart, Toronto, and by permission of the author.

"Mother Doesn't Want a Dog" from *If I Were in Charge of the World and Other Worries,* copyright ©1981 by Judith Viorst. Reprinted with permission of Atheneum Publishers, an imprint of Macmillan Publishing Company.

"Possibilities" from *At the Top of My Voice and Other Poems,* copyright ©1970 by Felice Holman. Reprinted with permission of Charles Scribner's Sons, an imprint of Macmillan Publishing Company.

A Special Trade by Sally Wittman with illustrations by Karen Gundersheimer, text copyright ©1978 by Sally Christensen Wittman, illustrations copyright ©1978 by Karen Gundersheimer. Reprinted by permission of Harper & Row, Publishers, Inc.

Contents

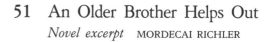

128   Touch the Sky

At the Top of My Voice

- from *Annabel Lee*, illustrated by Gilles Tibo

My Name Is Not Odessa Yarker

by Marian Engel
Illustrated by Maryann Kovalski

Geraldine Shingle was ten and her brother, Rufus, was nine. People thought they were twins because they were the same size. But they were not twins. Most of the time they did not even like each other.

He thought she was bossy and she thought he was a nuisance. He was always getting into her things. And he particularly wanted a share of the seven hundred and fifty-two jellybeans she had won in a contest at school. But Geraldine wanted to keep the jellybeans.

One Sunday Rufus told his father that he had decided to change his name. He thought the name José would be nice. But that wasn't all he changed the next day at school . . .

Just before recess, there was an announcement on the school intercom. "I would like your attention," said Mr. Bowron, the principal. "Rufus Shingle has an announcement to make."

In her classroom, Geraldine pricked up her ears. She had tried to pry Rufus's new name out of her father, without success. "Hi," said Rufus. "I just wanted to say this: My new name is José— that's J O S E, acute—pronounced Ho-*zay*. And," (very quickly now) "my sister, the jellybean hog, is now called Odessa Yarker." Click went the switch.

"What?" shouted Geraldine.

"Quiet, Odessa," said her teacher. "Line up for recess, class."

"Bbbut—," said Geraldine. . . .

"I think it's a very good idea," said the teacher. "Everyone needs a change every once in a while. I myself was once called Steele. I got married and changed my name to Wood. Now, Odessa, run on out with the others."

Geraldine couldn't believe what she had heard. Everyone was already calling her Odessa and not two minutes were up. It was a horrible name. It was the name of the worst baby-sitter they ever had. She was so angry with Rufus.

All the rest of the morning they called her Odessa. All afternoon, too. It made her feel mean, and it made her feel like crying. She told her teacher that she hated the name, and her teacher said mildly: "Is that so, Odessa? I think it's nice. It's Russian. There's a city in Russia called Odessa. You can look it up in the atlas."

By the time school was out, Geraldine felt awful. She tried to walk home alone, but a gang of Rufus's friends chased her yelling: "Ya, ya, Ode—ssa."

She wondered what to do when she went to school the next morning. She thought, Maybe they'll all have forgotten about it and I won't have to do anything. But she wasn't hopeful.

"Hi, Odessa," said Molly at the corner.

"My name is not Odessa Yarker."

"If you say so, Odessa."

When she got to the school, everyone was there and everyone called her Odessa. When it came time for their spelling test, she even found herself writing Odessa Yarker at the top of the page. I can't stand this, she thought. I'm turning into somebody else in front of my own eyes.

As soon as the test was over, she dropped her pencil and asked if she could leave the room. Then she did something she had never done before: instead of turning left to go to the washroom, she turned right and walked briskly out the school door.

There was no one in the park. She sat down on a bench to collect herself. She tried to think of some way to persuade them all that this was a terrible trick, and that she was not, would not be, and had never been called Odessa Yarker.

In the middle of the park there was a statue of a king on a horse. She had heard of this statue, but she had never seen it before. She went up to the statue and climbed on its plinth. Then she grabbed the horse's metal tail and climbed right up onto its back. She worked her way around into the king's lap.

She climbed up onto his shoulders. Then, balancing herself by grabbing his head, she stood fully upright with her legs astride and yelled and yelled at the world: "MY NAME IS NOT ODESSA YARKER."

Again and again she hollered her message. It made her feel good. The sound zoomed past the university, past the hospitals, out beyond the library, beyond the museums and the greenhouses. Her voice hammered the entire city.

People stared. Squirrels stopped chattering. Birds stopped singing. All the traffic in the circle stopped. Without looking at any of them, Geraldine climbed down the statue and walked quietly home.

She went into her room and sat down at her desk. TO WHOM IT MAY CONCERN: she wrote in big clear letters. MY NAME IS NOT ODESSA YARKER. MY DUMB BROTHER MADE THAT NAME UP FOR ME. I DO NOT ACCEPT HIS SUGGESTION. MY NAME IS AND ALWAYS WILL BE GERALDINE SHINGLE. (Signed) GERALDINE SHINGLE

She went down to her father's office and handed the letter to her father's secretary.

"I'd like six notarized copies, please," she said.

"Yes, Miss Geraldine," he said, and hurried away.

She took the copies to school without stopping for lunch. She did not need lunch. She gave copies of her statement to the principal, the vice-principal, Mrs. Wood, and her best friend, Molly. Then she went to Rufus's room. "I have an important message for my brother, José," she said.

When Rufus came to the door, she handed him the statement and he read it carefully. "You could have left out *dumb,*" he said.

"You could have left out Odessa Yarker."

"OK. I'm sorry. I didn't know it would be such a bad idea. Come on down to the principal's office."

The principal sighed, but he let them use the intercom again.

"This is José Shingle. I have an announcement to make," Rufus said. "My sister has brought in a legal notice. Her name is not Odessa Yarker. Her name is Geraldine Shingle, . . .

and to prove it, she's bringing seven hundred and fifty-two jellybeans to school. Goodbye."

Geraldine looked at him sourly. He had always been a smart aleck. But at least she had her own name back.

Outside the office, Rufus bent down for a drink at the water fountain. Geraldine looked at him and a crafty smile spread over her face. She shoved his face into the water, which went spurting into his ears.

"*Olé,* José," she said.

The Elephant Hunter

by Lorrie McLaughlin
Illustrated by Mike Martchenko

James was an elephant hunter, although no one would guess it just by looking at him.

Sometimes, people thought that there was something different about James, but they could never quite decide what it was.

"James!" his mother would say. "Stop staring into space and drink your milk."

When his mother said that, James would blink once and look at her with surprise. What was his mother doing there, with a glass of milk in her hands, surrounded by elephants?

When he blinked again, the elephants would go back into the jungle and he would say, "Yes, Ma'am," and drink his milk the way he was supposed to do.

"Don't worry so much about James," said his father, once or twice a day. "He'll be fine. He's just thinking."

When his father said that, James would blink once and try to look like somebody who was thinking, instead of like somebody who was hunting elephants.

Days when his mother and father didn't worry about whether he was staring into space or thinking, James went out into the jungle behind his house and hunted elephants from early in the morning until dinnertime.

Some days he hunted one or two, and some days he hunted as many as fifteen, and some days he didn't hunt any at all because all the elephants were off doing whatever elephants do when they are not being chased by an elephant hunter.

One morning James was lying on his back, under a maple tree, thinking about being an elephant hunter and looking at the sky, when he heard a rustling in the bushes behind him.

For a minute, he thought it might be an elephant or two. Then he remembered that elephants hardly ever made a rustling noise.

He sat up and looked around at two boys, one even smaller than he was and one a little bit bigger.

"Who are you and what are you doing?" demanded the bigger boy.

"I'm James, the elephant hunter," said James. And then he shut his mouth so tightly he almost bit his tongue. He hadn't meant to tell *anybody* that he was an elephant hunter. He knew that the minute he told anybody, nothing was ever quite the same.

The bigger boy just stared at him, but the boy who was even smaller than James began to giggle.

"An elephant hunter!" he said. "An elephant hunter!" He poked the bigger boy in the ribs. "An elephant hunter!"

The bigger boy didn't say anything at all. He kept right

on staring. Then he took the smaller boy by the arm and pulled him out of the yard, back to the sidewalk.

James stayed where he was, watching them walk down the street, the smaller boy still giggling and the bigger boy still not saying anything at all.

James sighed, finally. He lay down on the grass, staring up through the leaves to the blue sky.

The elephants were probably all gone, he decided. He probably wouldn't ever be an elephant hunter again.

He rolled over on his stomach and stared around his jungle. Over there by the garage he had hunted his very first elephant. And down by the lilac bush he had hunted at least three.

He looked at the garage and the lilac bush and waited. But no elephants came by. Not any at all. Not even when he waited for fifteen minutes.

James began untying and tying his shoelaces, wondering what he would do on Saturdays and holidays and warm summer evenings, now that there were no elephants left to hunt.

He tied two knots in one shoelace and wished that there was some way to call back words. If he hadn't told the boys he was an elephant hunter, things would be the same as they had always been.

He heard a rustling in the bushes behind him and tied a third knot in his shoelace. There was no use in turning around. No use at all. Elephants didn't rustle in bushes and even if they *did,* they would never come into his private jungle again.

James waited until the rustling had stopped. He turned around slowly and looked at the bigger boy.

"Where's your friend?" he said.

"He's my brother and he's home," said the bigger boy. He reached into a pocket and pulled out two crushed, dusty-looking doughnuts. He held one out to James.

James looked at it and then at the boy.

"Go on," said the bigger boy. "Take it." He shoved the doughnut across the grass toward James. He sat down on the grass beside him, eyes narrowed to slits. "We may have to wait a long time, you know," he said in a whisper. "Once elephants have been scared away by giggling, it takes a while for them to come back."

James took a small bite out of the doughnut. "Maybe all day," he said. "At least until sundown."

The bigger boy nodded his head. "Easily until sundown."

The two of them crouched in the grass, in the heart of the jungle, and waited, quietly, for the elephants to come.

Exploring an Underwater World

by Penny Howard
Photographs by
Fiona McCall

On August 28, 1988, an unusual sailboat named Lorcha *docked at Harbourfront in Toronto, Ontario. For five years,* Lorcha *had been home for Penny Howard and her younger brother, Peter, and their parents, Fiona and Paul, as they sailed from country to country around the world. The family had started out on their grand adventure on Penny's sixth birthday, July 1, 1983.*

When we left Canada, I knew how to swim, but I had never learned to dive or to snorkel, that is, to swim with a mask and breathing tube. I first wanted to snorkel on Bucco Reef in Tobago, an island in the clear, warm waters of the Caribbean.

Dad showed me how to put on a mask and snorkel. The mask keeps an airspace around your eyes, which enables you to see clearly through the water. The snorkel is simply a curved tube with a mouthpiece. You swim on the surface of the water with your face down and you breathe through the snorkel, which sticks up in the air above the water.

To tell you the truth, I was a little scared. What if I couldn't breathe? But when I looked out over the beautiful, warm, turquoise water, I decided it was too good a chance to miss, so I slipped in.

When I opened my eyes, I was in a different world. I was amazed at all the beautiful fish. Red and orange and green and blue and gold and purple creatures swam past, with all kinds of spots, dots, stripes, and squiggles.

But there were other, less friendly underwater creatures. When a mean-looking barracuda cruised by, I swam very close to Mom. He was almost two metres long!

Snorkelling on the surface of the water was fun, but soon I wanted to take a closer look at the fish and coral. So I began to learn to dive. The flippers I wore helped me swim faster and dive deeper. Soon I was diving down two or three metres.

Clarke Stede

Peter and I both liked to snorkel and to dive in the coral reefs and islands just off the coast of Venezuela. Sometimes we caught dinner for the whole family by diving for conch. These big shellfish are quite heavy, and Peter, only five, would be practically spluttering when he finally made it to the surface. Someone usually had to go and help him get the conch into the dinghy before he sank again under its weight.

If I had to select one favorite place to swim, it would be the Galapagos Islands in the Pacific Ocean. All the islands have very tame animals on them.

One day, our guide told us we could go swimming with the sea lions. I was a bit apprehensive about this. The slithery creatures looked quite friendly, but they were nearly as big as me and they were swimming around so fast. But after everyone else had slid into the water, I went in too. It was kind of fun, with sea lions zooming right at me, then sheering off at the very last moment, just centimetres away.

It was easier to make friends with the sea lions on shore than while swimming with them. I had a long talk with a sea lion who popped up out of the water beside a rock I was on. Another sea lion came ashore to tell Peter and me about how a shark had bitten off his flipper. He had nasty scars to back up his story.

By the time we got to the Solomon Islands in the South Pacific, I was a pretty strong swimmer and I felt comfortable diving to about three metres.

One day, someone from another boat asked Mom and Dad to dive for their "prop" (the propeller for the engine of their dinghy). They had dropped it overboard in about eight metres of water.

"There's also a really nice triton shell down there," said our friend.

"Hmmm," I thought to myself. I had never dived so deep before, but I took a long breath and swam down and down and down.

Everyone was surprised when I came up, gasping for breath—and holding the shell!

The shell now sits in my bedroom in Toronto. It reminds me of great adventures in faraway lands. It also tells me I can do whatever I want to do—if I just try.

Rosie and Michael

by Judith Viorst
Illustrated by Lorna Tomei

Rosie is my friend.

She likes me when I'm dopey and not just when I'm smart.

I worry a lot about pythons, and she understands.

My toes point in, and my shoulders droop, and there's hair growing out of my ears.

But Rosie says I look good.

She is my friend.

Michael is my friend.

He likes me when I'm grouchy
and not just when I'm nice.

I worry a lot about werewolves,
and he understands.
There's freckles growing all
over me, except on my
eyeballs and teeth.

But Michael says I look good.

He is my friend.

When I said that my nickname was Mickey, Rosie said Mickey. When I said that my nickname was Ace, Rosie said Ace. And when I was Tiger, and Lefty, and Ringo, Rosie always remembered.

That's how friends are.

When I wrote my name with a *y*, Michael wrote Rosey. When I wrote my name with an *i*, Michael wrote Rosi. And when I wrote Rosee, and Rozi, and Wrosie, Michael always did too.

That's how friends are.

Just because I sprayed Kool Whip in her sneakers, doesn't mean that Rosie's not my friend.

Just because I let the air out of his basketball, doesn't mean that Michael's not my friend.

When my parakeet died, I called Rosie.

When my bike got swiped, I called Rosie.

When I cut my head and the blood
came gushing out, as soon as the
blood stopped gushing, I called Rosie.

She is my friend.

When my dog ran away, I called
Michael. When my bike got swiped,
I called Michael. When I broke my
wrist and the bone was sticking
out, as soon as they stuck it back
in, I called Michael.

He is my friend.

Everybody Needs a Rock

by Byrd Baylor
Illustrated by Valerie Sinclair

Everybody
needs
a rock.

I'm sorry for kids
who don't have
a rock
for a friend.

I'm sorry for kids
who only have
TRICYCLES
BICYCLES
HORSES
ELEPHANTS
GOLDFISH
THREE-ROOM PLAYHOUSES
FIRE ENGINES
WIND-UP DRAGONS
AND THINGS LIKE THAT—
if
they don't have
a
rock
for a friend.

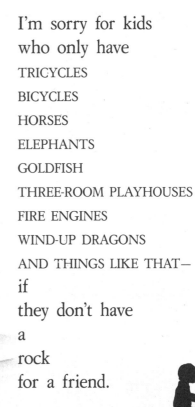

That's why
I'm giving them
my own
TEN RULES
for
finding
a
rock. . . .

Not
just
any rock.
I mean
a
special
rock
that you find
yourself
and keep
as long as
you can—
maybe
forever.

If somebody says,
"What's so special
about that rock?"
don't even tell them.
I don't.

Nobody
is supposed
to know
what's special
about
another person's
rock.

All right.
Here
are
the
rules:

RULE NUMBER 1

If you can,
go to a mountain
made out of
nothing but
a hundred million
small
shiny
beautiful
roundish
rocks.

But if you can't,
anyplace will do.
Even an alley.
Even a sandy road.

RULE NUMBER 2

When you are looking
at rocks
don't let
mothers or fathers
or sisters or brothers
or even best friends
talk
to you.
You should choose
a rock
when everything
is quiet.
Don't let dogs bark
at you
or bees buzz
at you.

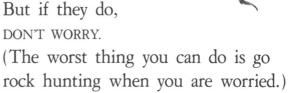

But if they do,
DON'T WORRY.
(The worst thing you can do is go
rock hunting when you are worried.)

RULE NUMBER 3

Bend over.
More.
Even more.
You may have to
sit
on the ground
with your head
almost
touching
the earth.
You have to look
a rock
right
in the eye.

Otherwise,
don't blame me
if you
can't find
a good one.

RULE NUMBER 4

Don't get a rock
that is
too big.
You'll
always
be sorry.
It won't fit
your hand
right
and it won't fit
your pocket.

A rock as big as
an apple
is too big.
A rock as big as
a horse
is
MUCH
too big.

RULE NUMBER 5

Don't choose a rock
that is
too small.
It will only be
easy
to lose
or
a mouse
might eat it,
thinking
that it
is a seed.

(Believe me,
that happened
to a boy
in the state
of Arizona.)

RULE NUMBER 6

The size
must be
perfect.
It has to feel
easy
in your hand
when you close
your fingers
over it.
It has to feel
jumpy
in your pocket
when you run.

Some people
touch
a rock
a thousand times
a day.
There aren't many things
that feel
as good as a rock—
if the rock
is
perfect.

RULE NUMBER 7

Look for
the perfect
color.
That could be
a sort of
pinkish gray
with bits of
silvery shine in it.
Some rocks
that look brown
are really other
colors,
but
you only see them
when you squint
and when the sun
is right.

Another way
to see colors
is to dip
your rock
in a clear mountain stream—
if one is passing by.

RULE NUMBER 8

The shape
of the rock
is up to you.
(There is a girl in Alaska
who only likes flat rocks.
Don't ask me why.
I like them lumpy.)

The thing to remember
about shapes
is this:
Any rock
looks good
with a hundred other rocks
around it on a hill.
But
if your rock
is going to be special
it should look good
by itself
in the bathtub.

RULE NUMBER 9

Always
sniff
a rock.
Rocks have
their own smells.
Some kids can tell
by sniffing
whether a rock
came from the middle
of the earth
or from an ocean
or from a mountain
where wind and sun
touched it
every day
for a million years.

You'll find out that grown-ups
can't tell these things.
Too bad for them.
They just can't smell as well
as kids can.

RULE NUMBER 10

Don't ask anybody
to help you choose.

I've seen
a lizard
pick one rock
out of
a desert full
of rocks
and go sit there
alone.
I've seen
a snail
pass up
twenty rocks
and spend all day
getting to
the one
it wanted.

You have to
make up
your own mind.
You'll
know.

All right,
that's
ten rules.
If you think
of any more
write them down
yourself.
I'm going out
to play a game
that takes
just me
and one rock
to play.

I happen to have
a rock here in my hand. . . .

Taking Care of
Crumley

by Ted Staunton
Illustrated by Tina Holdcroft

When it all began, I was hanging upside down. Suddenly the jungle gym shook. It got dark all around and I was looking at Ugly Augie Crumley and his Goons—the biggest bullies in school. Was I ever scared!

Ugly Augie smiled. He liked to scare kids. He pushed me, pinched me, poked me, pulled my ears, and just plain picked on me. Then they left me with my shoes tied to the bars and a promise to pick on me a whole lot more.

As soon as I got free, I went to see Maggie, the Greenapple Street Genius.

"Can you make Ugly Augie stop bugging me?" I asked. Maggie laughed. "No problem, Cyril. But . . . you'll have to do anything I say."

"No way!" I said. Then I remembered Ugly Augie's promise. "Okay," I sighed.

"Good," said Maggie. "Tomorrow I'll take care of Crumley. This is going to be fun!"

The next day was Friday. Maggie came down Greenapple Street and told me a Perfectly Perfect Plan. I had to tell a lie to Ugly Augie without anyone else hearing.

When I got to school, I snuck up to Ugly Augie and whispered, "Crumley, you're going to get it!" It felt nice to say.

A little louder I said, "My cousin Vern, who is in Grade 7 and plays football, is coming after school to make you into mush with one hand!" That felt even nicer.

I shouted, "He'll make you look like a hockey puck!" Then I roared, "You're all washed up, bozo!" and walked away like a big hero.

Maggie said that Ugly Augie was just a bully who was chicken inside. After school he would run home so fast that he'd never know I didn't have a cousin Vern. I thought my problem was solved.

Sure enough, after school I saw Ugly Augie sneaking off for home. Then I heard the Goons.

"Hey Augie, where are you going?"

"You can beat this guy!"

Now I knew why I was supposed to whisper—to keep the Goons away.

I got scared all over again. They came around the corner and saw me—all alone. I gulped. They charged, and I ran for my life.

Suddenly there was Maggie on her bike. "Hop on," she shouted, and we took off.

"You're gonna pay for lying to me, Cyril," yelled Ugly Augie. "Bring us money on Monday, or else!"

I told Maggie, "I forgot to whisper." She moaned. "My best plan ever and you blew it, Cyril. Now I have to start all over, and you have to carry my books. And watch out for the poison ivy around here."

We went home to Greenapple Street and didn't say another word.

I worried all weekend while Maggie sat in her tree thinking. At last, on Sunday, she came down. She was dressed very strangely.

"Cyril," she said, "I have a Terribly Terrific Plan. Open your piggy bank and put all your pennies in this bag."

When I was done, she took the bag and headed down the street. "See you tomorrow," was all she said.

Monday morning Maggie was ready. "Here's the plan," she said. "Tell Ugly Augie you have poison ivy. Then try to give him the bag of pennies. He'll be scared to touch you or your money ever again."

"Not another lie," I groaned. "I don't even have poison ivy."

"No, dummy," said Maggie, "but I'll make you look like you do." When she was finished, Maggie smiled. "You sure look sick," she said. "Now go do your stuff."

I started to walk, but my knees were knocking. Every penny I owned was in that bag. What if I didn't fool them?

I peeked around the corner. Ugly Augie looked awfully ugly that morning. The Goons looked like grumpy gorillas. I got goose bumps all over.

I opened the bag and stuffed some money in my shirt, just in case. Then I walked out to the jungle gym.

Slowly they circled me. My stomach got all squishy. Ugly Augie smiled and said, "Gimme."

"H-h-here," I said. "But I have poison ivy and if you touch me or my stuff you'll get it too!"

Ugly Augie stared. Then he rubbed my face. "Lipstick," he snorted. "This kid always lies." He snatched my money and in a second they all had some.

The Terribly Terrific Plan had turned terrifically terrible.

But when I ran back to Maggie and told her what had happened, she began to laugh. "It worked, it worked," she whooped. "I knew they'd take the money!"

"What?" I said.

"Yesterday I took your pennies to the field and mushed them up with poison ivy," she said. "Augie and his Goons are going to itch like crazy. And they'll be scared to touch you in case they get even more. I've taken care of Crumley!"

"All right!" I roared, and we danced around. After a minute, I stopped. I felt itchy. Maggie scratched her hands. Then I remembered.

"Oh, no," I said.

Slowly I felt inside my shirt. "I kept some of the money," I whispered.

"Eeeek," screeched Maggie. "You dummy. We have poison ivy!"

We itched for a month. Everybody got in trouble for what they did to everybody else, and everybody blamed me.

One day I met Ugly Augie on Greenapple Street. "Oh, oh," I thought, but he ran away.

"You keep away from me, Cyril," he yelled.

I went to the schoolyard. A couple of the Goons were there, but they hid when they saw me.

"Quit picking on us, Cyril," they shouted.

Suddenly everything was all right. Maggie's plan had worked. Ugly Augie had stopped bugging me. We had taken care of Crumley!

The Pain

by *Judy Blume*
Illustrated by Phillipe Beha

My brother's a pain.
He won't get out of bed
In the morning.
Mom has to carry him
Into the kitchen.
He opens his eyes
When he smells
His corn flakes.

He should get dressed
    himself.
He's six.
He's in first grade.
But he's so pokey
Daddy has to help him
Or he'd never be ready
    in time
And he'd miss the bus.

He cries if I
Leave without him.
Then Mom gets mad
And yells at me
Which is another
  reason why
My brother's a pain.

He's got to be first
To show Mom
His school work.
She says *ooh* and *aah*
Over all his pictures
Which aren't great at all
But just ordinary
First grade stuff.

When he takes a bath
My brother the pain
Powders the whole bathroom
And never gets his face clean.
Daddy says
He's learning to
Take care of himself.
I say,
He's a slob!

My brother the pain
Is two years younger than me.
So how come
He gets to stay up
As late as I do?
Which isn't really late enough
For somebody in third grade
Anyway.

I asked Mom and
　Daddy about that.
They said,
"You're right.
You *are* older.
You *should* stay
　up later."

So they tucked the Pain
Into bed.
I couldn't wait
For the fun to begin.
I waited
And waited
And waited.

But Daddy and Mom
Just sat there
Reading books.

Finally I shouted,
"I'm going to bed!"

"We thought you wanted
To stay up later,"
They said.

"I did.
But without the Pain
There's nothing to do!"

"Remember that tomorrow,"
Mom said.
And she smiled.

But the next day
My brother was
   a pain again.
When I got a phone call
He danced all around me
Singing stupid songs
At the top of his lungs.
Why does he have to
   act that way?

And why does he
   always
Want to be
   garbage man
When I build a city
Out of blocks?
Who needs him
Knocking down
   buildings
With his dumb
   old trucks!

And I would really like to know
Why the cat sleeps on the Pain's bed
Instead of mine
Especially since I am the one
Who feeds her.
That is the meanest thing of all!

I don't understand
How Mom can say
The Pain is lovable.
She's always kissing him
And hugging him
And doing disgusting things
Like that.
And Daddy says
The Pain is just what
They always wanted.

YUCK!

I think they love him better than me.

An Older Brother Helps Out

by Mordecai Richler
Illustrated by Sharon Matthews

When he was six years old, a mere child, he was known as Jacob Two-Two. He was given the name because he was two plus two plus two years old. He had two ears and two eyes and two feet and two shoes. He also had two older brothers, Daniel and Noah, and two older sisters, Emma and Marfa. But most of all, he was given the name because, as Jacob Two-Two himself once admitted, "I am the littlest in our family. Nobody hears what I say the first time. They only pay attention if I say things two times."

from Jacob Two-Two and the Dinosaur

But now that he was eight years old he felt that he was too grown up to go by such a childish name. All the same, it stuck to him. After all, he still had two older brothers and two older sisters. And, as they were quick to point out, if he had once been two plus two plus two years old, he was now—come to think of it—only two times two times two years old. Not much of a difference, they said, but they really didn't understand.

Jacob Two-Two had learned a good deal since he had been a mere six years old. He could now dial a telephone number, do joined-up writing of a sort, and catch a ball, providing Noah wasn't aiming it bang at his head. True, his two older brothers and his two older sisters were still taller and much more capable than he was. And snootier than ever, it sometimes seemed to him.

Marfa, for instance, who was only four years older than Jacob Two-Two, no longer allowed him into the bathroom with her. "I know you're too young and stupid to understand," she said, "but it just isn't right for you to take a shower with me anymore."

Even so, some things were looking up. Jacob Two-Two could now cut a slice of bread that wasn't a foot thick on one end and thin as a sheet of paper on the other—unless Emma gave him a poke at just the right moment and then squealed, "Oh, Mummy, I don't want to make any trouble, but look what the baby of the family just did to the last loaf of bread in the house."

School was also a problem. A big problem.

When Jacob Two-Two had been a mere six years old, the family had lived in a big rambling old house on Kingston Hill in England. A year later his father had moved them all to Montreal, Canada, where he had come from in the first place. This was a great hardship for Jacob Two-Two, because the kids at his new school in Montreal poked fun at his British accent. The trouble-maker-in-chief was fat Freddy Jackson. He would gather together a bunch of the other kids and then corner Jacob Two-Two in the schoolyard. "Hey, Jacob," he'd say, "what does your father put in his car to make it run?"

"Petrol," Jacob Two-Two would reply. "Petrol." Because when he was nervous or excited he still said many things two times.

"That's what they call gasoline over in stinky old England," Freddy would explain, even as the other kids had begun to giggle. Then, turning to Jacob Two-Two again, he would ask, "And what are we standing on right now?"

"The grahs."

Soon enough, however, Jacob Two-Two learned to say "gasoline" when what he really meant was "petrol." Practising in front of a mirror, he even taught himself to say "grass" instead of "grahs."

Unfortunately, everybody in the family picked on Jacob Two-Two too. If, for instance, he came home from school in a cheerful mood and called out, "Am I ever starved! What's for dinner?" Noah was bound to leap up, make a frightening face, and say, "Dead cow."

Once he came home from school and asked his father for a measly dollar so that he could go to the movies on Saturday morning. Noah, as usual, had to put in his two cents. "You can't give the child a dollar just like that," he said. "It would be spoiling him." (But Noah wasn't all bad. He often allowed Jacob Two-Two to tag along with him on his newspaper route. In fact, he actually allowed Jacob Two-Two to deliver the newspaper himself to any house with a sign that warned BEWARE OF THE DOG.)

"Your brother has a point, Jacob. You will have to win the money by proving your intelligence. Now then, are you ready for a quiz?"

"Yes," Jacob Two-Two said. "Yes, I am!"

"Good. Now you will have to concentrate, because I can allow you only five seconds on the first impossibly difficult question. Ready?"

"Ready!"

"Okay. Here we go. For a big fifty cents tell me how long was the Seven Years War?"

"Seven years!"

"Excellent! Brilliant! Now, watch out for the next question because it is about the kings of France. Ready?"

"Yes."

"Good. Here it comes. For another fifty cents tell me what Louis came after Louis the Fourteenth?"

"Louis the Fifteenth."

"Wow! You're really flying today, kid. You have won a dollar," his father said, handing it over. "Now, are you a chicken-livered, trembling coward, or would you like to try another question—a really easy one—for one thousand dollars?"

"Yes! Yes! I'll try it."

"All right, then. Here it is. Jacob Two-Two, for one

thousand dollars cash, tell me how you spell 'chrysanthemum.' "

Jacob Two-Two groaned. Why, he thought, was everybody in the house always teasing him? Everybody. One day, sure enough, it got him into trouble at school, but that was Daniel's fault, teasing again. Jacob Two-Two had been lying on the living-room carpet showing off that he was now old enough to have homework to do in his very own assignment book. Looking up from the book, he asked, "Does anybody know what 'denote' means?"

Daniel told him what it meant, but Jacob Two-Two should have guessed that something was up, because no sooner did Daniel explain the word than Emma hid her face in a pillow. Noah burst out laughing. Marfa whispered, "Hey, Daniel, you shouldn't have said that. He's just dumb enough to repeat it at school."

Actually Jacob Two-Two hardly ever spoke up in class, because he was still ashamed of his British accent. This worried his schoolteacher, Miss Sour Pickle. First thing at school the next morning, Miss Pickle turned to Jacob Two-Two. "Jacob, would you please stand up and tell the rest of the class the meaning of the word 'denote.' "

"Yes, Miss Pickle." And, remembering what Daniel had taught him, Jacob Two-Two said, "Denote is what you write with de pencil and de paper."

Everybody in the class began to laugh, except for Miss Pickle. "Well, I never!" she said. "What cheekiness! How very, very rude! Jacob, you go stand in the corner at once, and after class is out this afternoon you will stay behind to wash all the blackboards."

When Jacob Two-Two finally got out of school late that afternoon, the other kids were waiting for him. But they hadn't stayed behind to tease him about his British accent. Instead they wanted to be friends. All of them. Even fat Freddy.

Jacob Two-Two was thrilled. Things were working out for him in Montreal at last.

Mother Doesn't Want a Dog

by Judith Viorst
Illustrated by Jock McCrae

Mother doesn't want a dog.
Mother says they smell,
And never sit when you say sit,
Or even when you yell.
And when you come home late at night
And there is ice and snow,
You have to go back out because
The dumb dog has to go.

Mother doesn't want a dog.
Mother says they shed,
And always let the strangers in
And bark at friends instead,
And do disgraceful things on rugs,
And track mud on the floor,
And flop upon your bed at night
And snore their doggy snore.

Mother doesn't want a dog.
She's making a mistake.
Because, more than a dog, I think
She will not want this snake.

Possibilities

by Felice Holman
Illustrated by Jackie Snider

Possibilities, possibilities, possibilities, possibilities.
"Yes" is best, "Yes" is best,
But next to that is "Maybe."
"We'll see" can sometimes grow to "Yes,"
But when they say "I doubt it"
You're on the way to no.
And next they say, "I don't think so";
And finally it's "No,"
And finally it's "No."
"I don't think so,"
"I don't think so,"
Down
Down
Down.
There's nowhere else to go
But frown
And then say "No."

Im-possibilities, Im-possibilities, "No."

A Special Trade

by Sally Wittman
Illustrated by Karen Gundersheimer

Old Bartholomew is Nelly's neighbor.

When Nelly was very small, he would take her every day for a walk down the block to Mrs. Pringle's vegetable garden.

Bartholomew never pushed too fast. He always warned Nelly about Mr. Oliver's bumpy driveway: "Hang on, Nell! Here's a bump!" And she'd shout "BUMP!" as she rode over it.

If they met a nice dog along the way, they'd stop and pet it. But if it was nasty, Bartholomew would shoo it away.

When Mrs. Pringle's sprinkler was on, he would say, "Get ready, get set, CHAAARRRRRRRRRRRRRGE!" Nelly would squeal "Wheeeee!" as he pushed her through it.

When Nelly began to walk, Bartholomew took her by the hand. "NO-NO!" she cried, pulling it back.

Nelly didn't want any help.

So Bartholomew offered his hand only when she really needed it.

Bartholomew was getting older, too. He needed a walking stick. So they walked very slowly. When they walked upstairs, they *both* held on to the railing.

The neighbors called them "ham and eggs" because they were always together.

Even on Hallowe'en.

And on the coldest day of winter when everyone else was inside.

One summer Bartholomew taught Nelly to skate by circling his walking stick. "Easy does it!" he warned.

Then she skated right over his toes! He wasn't mad, though. He just whistled and rubbed his foot.

The first time Nelly tried to skate by herself,

she fell.

Bartholomew saw that she felt like crying. He pulled up something from the garden and said, "Don't be saddish, have a radish!"

Nelly laughed and ate it. She didn't really like radishes, but she did like Bartholomew.

Before long, Nelly was in school and Bartholomew had gotten even older.

Sometimes he needed a helping hand, but he didn't like to take one.

So Nelly held out her hand only when Bartholomew really needed it.

Whenever Bartholomew had to stop and rest, Nelly would beg for a story about the "old days."

Once after a story, she asked him, "Will we ever run out of things to talk about?"

"If we do," said Bartholomew, "we just won't say anything. Good friends can do that."

Some days they just took it easy and sat on the porch. Bartholomew would play a tune on his harmonica. Nelly would make up the words.

One day Bartholomew went out alone and fell down the stairs. An ambulance with a red flasher and a siren took him to the hospital.

He was gone for a long time.

Nelly wrote him every day. She always ended with, "Come back soon, so we can go for walks again."

When Bartholomew came home, he was in a wheelchair. The smile was gone from his eyes.

"I guess our walks are over," he said.

"No they aren't," said Nelly. "*I* can take *you* for walks now."

She knew just how to do it, too.

Nice and easy, not too fast.

Just before Mr. Oliver's driveway, she would call, "Get ready for the bump!" And Bartholomew would wave his hat like a cowboy as he rode over it.

If they saw a nice dog, they'd stop and pet it.

But if it was mean, Nelly would shoo it away.

One day when the sprinkler was on, Nelly started to go around. But she changed her mind. "All right, Bartholomew.

Ready, set, one, two, three. CHAAARRRRRRRRRRRRRGE!"
And she pushed him right through it!

"Ah . . . that was fun!" said Bartholomew.

Nelly grinned. "I hope your wheelchair won't rust."

"Fiddlesticks!" He laughed. "Who cares if it does!"

Mrs. Pringle leaned over the fence.
"Seems just like yesterday Bartholomew
was pushing *you* in the stroller."

"That was when I was little,"
said Nelly. "Now it's my
turn to push and
Bartholomew's turn
to sit . . . kind of
like a trade."

Then they sat
in the sun to dry.
Nelly munched
on a carrot.
Bartholomew played a tune on his harmonica.

Nelly could see the old smile was back in Bartholomew's
eyes.

Words,
Words,
Words

from *Abiyoyo*, illustrated by Michael Hays

Sam, Bangs & MOONSHINE

Written and illustrated by Evaline Ness

On a small island, near a large harbor, there once lived a fisherman's little daughter (named Samantha, but always called Sam), who had the reckless habit of lying.

Not even the sailors home from the sea could tell stranger stories than Sam. Not even the ships in the harbor, with curious cargoes from giraffes to gerbils, claimed more wonders than Sam did.

Sam said her mother was a mermaid, when everyone knew she was dead.

Sam said she had a fierce lion at home, and a baby kangaroo. (Actually, what she *really* had was an old wise cat called Bangs.)

Sam even said that Bangs could talk if and when he wanted to.

Sam said this. Sam said that. But whatever Sam said you could never believe.

Even Bangs yawned and shook his head when she said the ragged old rug on the doorstep was a chariot drawn by dragons.

Early one morning, before Sam's father left in his fishing boat to be gone all day, he hugged Sam hard and said, "Today, for a change, talk REAL not MOONSHINE. MOONSHINE spells trouble."

Sam promised. But while she washed the dishes, made the beds, and swept the floor, she wondered what he meant. When she asked Bangs to explain REAL and MOONSHINE, Bangs jumped on her shoulder and purred, "MOONSHINE is flummadiddle. REAL is the opposite."

Sam decided that Bangs made no sense whatever.

When the sun made a golden star on the cracked window, Sam knew it was time to expect Thomas.

Thomas lived in the tall grand house on the hill. Thomas had two cows in the barn, twenty-five sheep, a bicycle with a basket, and a jungle-gym on the lawn. But most important of all, Thomas believed every word Sam said.

At the same time every day Thomas rode his bicycle down the hill to Sam's house and begged to see her baby kangaroo.

Every day Sam told Thomas it had just "stepped out." She sent Thomas everywhere to find it. She sent him to the tallest trees where, she said, it was visiting owls. Or perhaps it was up in the old windmill, grinding corn for its evening meal.

"It might be," said Sam, "in the lighthouse tower, warning ships at sea."

"Or maybe," she said, "it's asleep on the sand. Somewhere, anywhere on the beach."

Wherever Sam sent Thomas, he went. He climbed up trees, ran down steps, and scoured the beach, but he never found Sam's baby kangaroo.

While Thomas searched, Sam sat in her chariot and was drawn by dragons to faraway secret worlds.

Today, when Thomas arrived, Sam said, "That baby kangaroo just left to visit my mermaid mother. She lives in a cave behind Blue Rock."

Sam watched Thomas race away on his bicycle over the narrow strand that stretched to a massive blue rock in the distance. Then she sat down in her chariot. Bangs came out of the house and sat down beside Sam. With his head turned in the direction of the diminishing Thomas, Bangs said, "When the tide comes up, it covers the road to Blue Rock. Tide rises early today."

Sam looked at Bangs for a minute. Then she said, "Pardon me while I go to the moon."

Bangs stood up. He stretched his front legs. Then he stretched his back legs. Slowly he stalked away from Sam toward Blue Rock.

Suddenly Sam had no desire to go to the moon. Or any other place either. She just sat in her chariot and thought about Bangs and Thomas.

She was so busy thinking that she was unaware of thick muddy clouds that blocked out the sun. Nor did she hear the menacing rumble of thunder. She was almost knocked off the doorstep when a sudden gust of wind drove torrents of rain against her face.

Sam leaped into the house and slammed the door. She went to the window to look at Blue Rock, but she could see nothing through the gray ribbed curtain of rain. She wondered where Thomas was. She wondered where Bangs was. Sam stood there looking at nothing, trying to swallow the lump that rose in her throat.

The murky light in the room deepened to black. Sam was still at the window when her father burst into the house. Water streamed from his hat and oozed from his boots. Sam ran to him screaming, "Bangs and Thomas are out on the rock! Blue Rock! Bangs and Thomas!"

As her father turned quickly and ran out the door, he ordered Sam to stay in the house.

"And pray that the tide hasn't covered the rock!" he yelled.

When her father had gone, Sam sat down. She listened to the rain hammer on the tin roof. Then suddenly it stopped.

Sam closed her eyes and mouth, tight. She waited in the quiet room. It seemed to her that she waited forever.

At last she heard her father's footsteps outside. She flung open the door and said one word: "Bangs?"

Sam's father shook his head.

"He was washed away," he said. "But I found Thomas on the rock. I brought him back in the boat. He's home now, safe in bed. Can you tell me how all this happened?"

Sam started to explain, but sobs choked her. She cried so hard that it was a long time before her father understood everything.

Finally, Sam's father said, "Go to bed now. But before you go to sleep, Sam, tell yourself the difference between REAL and MOONSHINE."

Sam went to her room and crept into bed. With her eyes wide open she thought about REAL and MOONSHINE.

MOONSHINE was a mermaid-mother, a fierce lion, a chariot drawn by dragons, and certainly a baby kangaroo. It was all flummadiddle just as Bangs had told her. Or *had* he told her? Wouldn't her father say that a cat's talking was MOONSHINE?

REAL was no mother at all. REAL was her father and Bangs. And now there wasn't even Bangs. Tears welled up in Sam's eyes again. They ran down into her ears making a scratching noise. Sam sat up and blew her nose. The scratching was not in her ears. It was at the window. As Sam stared at the black oblong, two enormous yellow eyes appeared and stared back. Sam sprang from her bed and opened the window. There sat Bangs, his coat a sodden mess.

"Oh, Bangs!" cried Sam, as she grabbed and smothered him with kisses. "What happened to you?"

In a few words Bangs told her that one moment he was on the rock with Thomas and the next he was lying at the foot of the lighthouse tower two kilometres away. All done by waves.

"Nasty stuff, water," Bangs grumbled, as he washed himself from his ears to his feet.

Sam patted Bangs. "Well, at least it's not flummadiddle. . . ." Sam paused. She looked up to see her father standing in the doorway.

"Look! Bangs is home!" shouted Sam.

"Hello, Bangs. What's not flummadiddle?" asked Sam's father.

"Bangs! And you! And Thomas!" answered Sam. "Oh, Daddy! I'll always know the difference between REAL and MOONSHINE now. Bangs and Thomas were almost lost because of MOONSHINE. Bangs told me."

"He *told* you?" questioned Sam's father.

"Well, he would have *if* he could talk," said Sam. Then she added sadly, "I know cats can't talk like people, but I almost believed I *did* have a baby kangaroo."

Her father looked steadily at her.

"There's good MOONSHINE and bad MOONSHINE," he said. "The important thing is to know the difference." He kissed Sam good night and left the room.

When he had closed the door, Sam said, "You know, Bangs, I might just keep my chariot."

This time Bangs did not yawn and shake his head. Instead he licked her hand. He waited until she got into bed, then he curled up at her feet and went to sleep.

The next morning Sam opened her eyes to see an incredible thing! Hopping toward her on its hind legs was a small, elegant, large-eyed animal with a long tail like a lion's. Behind it strolled Bangs and her father.

"A baby kangaroo!" shouted Sam. "Where did you find it!"

"It is *not* a baby kangaroo," said Sam's father. "It's a gerbil. I found it on an African banana boat in the harbor."

"Now Thomas can see a baby kangaroo at last!" Sam squealed with joy.

Sam's father interrupted her. "Stop the MOONSHINE, Sam. Call it by its REAL name. Anyway, Thomas won't come today. He's sick in bed with laryngitis. He can't even talk. Also his bicycle got lost in the storm."

Sam looked down at the gerbil. Gently she stroked its tiny head. Without raising her eyes, she said, "Daddy, do you think I should *give* the gerbil to Thomas?"

Sam's father said nothing. Bangs licked his tail.

Suddenly Sam hollered, "Come on, Bangs!"

She jumped out of bed and slipped into her shoes. As she grabbed her coat, she picked up the gerbil and ran from the house with Bangs at her heels. Sam did not stop running until she stood at the side of Thomas's bed.

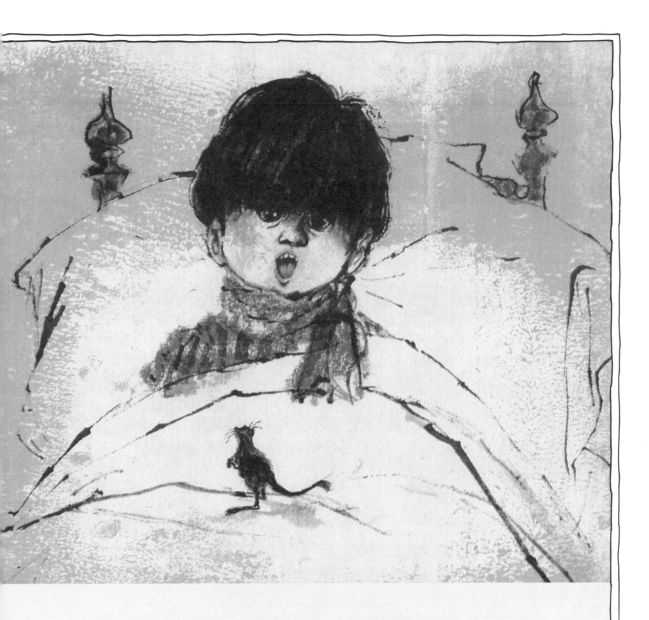

Very carefully she placed the gerbil on Thomas's stomach.
The little animal sat straight up on its long hind legs and
gazed directly at Thomas with its immense round eyes.

"Whaaaaaaaaaa sis name!" wheezed Thomas.

"MOONSHINE," answered Sam, as she gave Bangs a big
wide smile.

Animals Together

Written and illustrated by Nicola Morgan

When Lordly and Loving Lions
Get together
They become a PRIDE

A Pride of Lions

from Pride of Lions

When Cross and
Cranky Camels
Get together
They become a
TRAIN

A Train of Camels

When Fat and
　　Fanciful Fish
　　　　Get together
　　　　　　They become a
　　　　　　　　SCHOOL

A School of Fish

When Large
Lovely Leopards
Get together
They become a
LEAP

A Leap of Leopards

Written and illustrated by Barbara Bottner

89

90

Do You Really Mean It?

by Marvin Terban

In one ear and out the other

MEANING:
Going through the mind without leaving an impression

There's plenty inside a person's head. Nothing could really go "in one ear and out the other." But if someone isn't paying attention to what is being said, then words do seem to pass right through that person's head without being heard.

To take the words right out of someone's mouth

MEANING:
To say exactly what someone was just going to say

Suppose you're thinking, It's a beautiful day, and you're just going to say, It's a beautiful day, but before you do, someone else says, "It's a beautiful day." That person took the words right out of your mouth.

from In a Pickle

Your eyes are bigger than your stomach.

MEANING:
You ask for a lot of food, but then you can't eat it all.

In real life, of course, your stomach is much, much bigger than your eyes. But suppose you ask for all this food: two hot dogs, a slice of pizza, a glass of soda (pop), a bag of popcorn, an ice-cream cone, and a large chocolate doughnut. It looks good. But you can't possibly finish all that because your stomach is full. You would realize what it means when someone says, "Your eyes are bigger than your stomach."

To put your foot into your mouth

MEANING:
To say something that you shouldn't have said

If you don't watch where you're walking, you could put your foot right into something disagreeable. If you don't watch what you're saying, you could say something that might offend someone.

Naturally your foot wouldn't actually be inside your mouth when you were committing this social blunder. But the idea is the same. Your mouth is where the unpleasant words came from, and because you weren't careful, you "put your foot" right into it.

To get into everyone's hair

MEANING:
To keep bothering people

If something got into your hair—gum, sticky candy, paint, spaghetti sauce, glue—it would be hard to get out, and you certainly would be annoyed.

You can "get into someone's hair" when you keep bothering a person, even if he is bald!

Don't cry over spilled milk.

MEANING:
It's useless to cry about what can't be undone.

If you knock over a glass of milk, crying might make you feel better, but your tears won't get the milk back into the glass.

If something bad happens and there's no way to make it right again, tears are sometimes a comfort, but they aren't a solution to the problem.

To get up on the wrong side of the bed

MEANING:
To be grumpy

The ancient Romans were very superstitious. They thought it was extremely unlucky to get out of bed on the left side.

(The Latin word for *left* is *sinister*, which means "bad" or "evil.")

The right side of the bed was the safe, correct side. So if you absentmindedly got out on the left side, you would probably have a terribly unlucky day. That would certainly put you into a nasty mood, wouldn't it?

Play Ball,
Amelia Bedelia

by Peggy Parish
Illustrated by Wallace Tripp

"Here she is! Here's Amelia Bedelia!" called the Grizzlies.
"Then let's play ball," said the Tornados.
"The Tornados are up first," said Tom. "Amelia Bedelia, you stand here. Catch the ball if it comes your way."
"All right," she said.
"Batter up!" called the pitcher. The pitcher threw the ball. The batter hit it. He ran to first base.

"Get the ball, Amelia Bedelia," yelled Tom. "Tag Jack before he gets to second base."

"I must have a tag in here somewhere," said Amelia Bedelia. She tagged Jack.

Another boy came up to bat. He hit the ball. The ball landed near Amelia Bedelia.

"Throw it to first base," yelled the boys. "Put Dick out." So Amelia Bedelia threw the ball to first base.

Then she ran and grabbed Dick. "How far out do you want him?" she called.

"Amelia Bedelia!" shouted the boys. "Put him down."

So Amelia Bedelia put Dick down. "You sure do change your minds fast," she said. "You told me to put him out!"

Dick got back on first base. And the game went on. The next batter missed the ball. The catcher threw the ball to the pitcher. The pitcher missed it. But Amelia Bedelia caught it!

"Hurry, Amelia Bedelia! Throw the ball!" shouted the boys. "Dick is trying to steal second base."

"Steal second base!" said Amelia Bedelia. "That's not nice."

Amelia Bedelia ran and picked up second base. "It's all right now, fellows," she called. "Second base is safe."

"For gosh sakes, Amelia Bedelia!" said the boys. "Put that back."

Amelia Bedelia looked puzzled. "But he was going to steal it," she said.

"It's all right to steal bases," said Tom. "That is part of the game."

"Oh!" said Amelia Bedelia.

Finally the Tornados were out. They had made two runs.
It was the Grizzlies' turn at bat.

Tom was first. He struck out.

Then Jimmy had his turn. He hit that ball hard. He
made it to third base.

Next it was Bob's turn. He hit the ball.

"Pop fly," called the pitcher. "I've got it."

"Pop fly?" said Amelia Bedelia. "I didn't hear anything
pop!"

Then it was Amelia Bedelia's turn.

"Come on, Amelia Bedelia," said Bob. "Make a base hit so Jimmy can come in."

"Which base should I hit?" she asked.

Tom said, "Just hit that ball and run to first base!"

"All right," said Amelia Bedelia. And that is just what she did.

Jimmy scored for the Grizzlies. The team cheered. The next player struck out. The Tornados were at bat again.

The score was Tornados 2, Grizzlies 1. The Grizzlies called a time-out.

"Amelia Bedelia is not very good in the field," said Jimmy.

"She gets all mixed up," said Tom.

"Maybe she could be catcher," said Bob.

The boys turned to Amelia Bedelia. "You be the catcher," said Jimmy.

"What do I do?" she asked.

"Stand behind the batter and catch the ball," said Jimmy. "Then throw it back to the pitcher."

So Amelia Bedelia stood behind the batter. The pitcher threw the ball. The batter was about to hit it. But Amelia Bedelia pushed him out of the way.

And Amelia Bedelia caught the ball. "I got it, fellows!" she called. The whole team groaned. The Tornados were very angry.

"Put her someplace else," they shouted. "Put her way out."

So the Grizzlies put Amelia Bedelia way out in the field.

The game was not going well for the Grizzlies. The score was Tornados 8, Grizzlies 5.

The Grizzlies were at bat. It was the last inning. They had two outs. The bases were loaded. And Amelia Bedelia was at bat.

The Grizzlies were worried. "Please, Amelia Bedelia," they said. "Please hit that ball hard."

Amelia Bedelia swung at the first ball. She missed.

She swung at the second ball. And again she missed.

"Please, Amelia Bedelia, please," shouted the Grizzlies.

Amelia Bedelia swung at the next ball. And oh, how she hit that ball!

"Run, Amelia Bedelia, run!" yelled the boys. "Run to first base." And Amelia Bedelia ran.

"Tom says stealing is all right," she said, "so I'll just steal all the bases. I will make sure the Grizzlies win."

Amelia Bedelia scooped up first base, and second base, and third base.

"Home!" shouted the boys. "Run home, Amelia Bedelia!"

Amelia Bedelia looked puzzled, but she did not stop running. And on her way she scooped up home plate too.

The boys were too surprised to say a thing. Then Tom yelled, "We won! We won the game!"

"Amelia Bedelia, come back!" shouted the boys. "We won!"

But Amelia Bedelia was running too fast to hear. She did not stop until she reached home.

"That is a silly game," she said. "Having me run all the way home!"

Suddenly she heard a loud roar. "Hurray! Hurray! Hurray for Amelia Bedelia!" There were the Grizzlies.

"We won! The score was Grizzlies 9, Tornados 8," said Jimmy. "You saved the game, Amelia Bedelia."

"I'm glad I could help you boys out," said Amelia Bedelia.

A Twist of Tongues

Illustrated by Carlos Freire

Bike-Twister

by Dennis Lee

Place a foot upon a pedal,
Put your pedal-pushers on;
To the pedal pin a paddle,
Paddle-pedal push upon.

Place the paddle-pedal-cycle
On a puddle in the park;
Paddle addled through the puddle,
Pump the pedal till it's dark.

On the puddle-pedal-paddler
Place a poodle with a pail:
Let the addled paddle-pedaller's
Puddle-poodle bail.

Eletelephony

by Laura E. Richards

Once there was an elephant,
Who tried to use the telephant—
No! No! I mean an elephone
Who tried to use the telephone—
(Dear me! I am not certain quite
That even now I've got it right.)

Howe'er it was, he got his trunk
Entangled in the telephunk;
The more he tried to get it free,
The louder buzzed the telephee—
(I fear I'd better drop the song
Of elephop and telephong!)

Mabel Murple

by Sheree Fitch

Mabel Murple's house was purple
So was Mabel's hair
Mabel Murple's cat was purple
Purple everywhere.

Mabel Murple's bike was purple
So were Mabel's ears
And when Mabel Murple cried
She cried terrible purple tears.

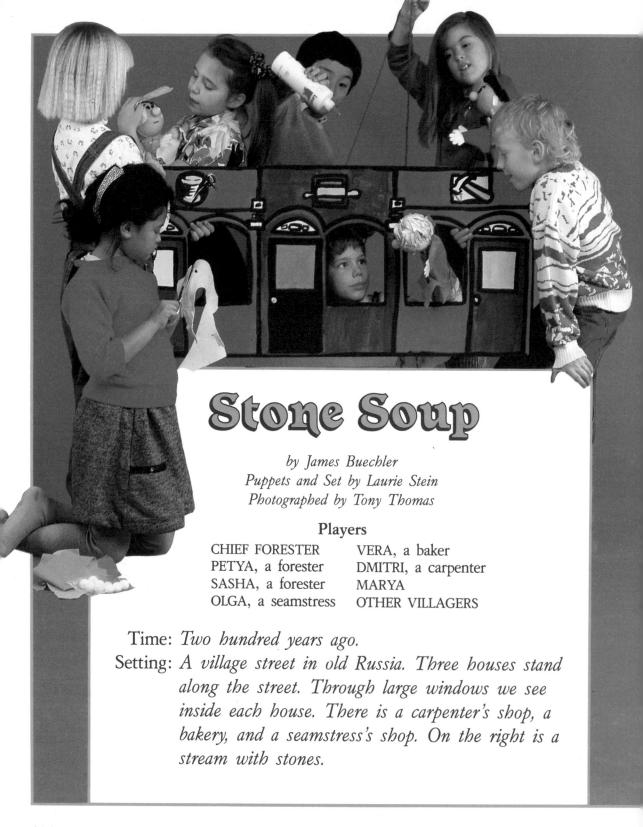

Stone Soup

by James Buechler
Puppets and Set by Laurie Stein
Photographed by Tony Thomas

Players

CHIEF FORESTER	VERA, a baker
PETYA, a forester	DMITRI, a carpenter
SASHA, a forester	MARYA
OLGA, a seamstress	OTHER VILLAGERS

Time: *Two hundred years ago.*

Setting: *A village street in old Russia. Three houses stand along the street. Through large windows we see inside each house. There is a carpenter's shop, a bakery, and a seamstress's shop. On the right is a stream with stones.*

Scene One

Dmitri is at work in the carpenter's shop. Vera works in the bakery kitchen. Olga sits sewing in the seamstress's shop. Three foresters enter and walk down the street. Chief Forester carries an axe. Petya has a knapsack. Sasha carries a large cooking pot.

CHIEF FORESTER: *(To Petya and Sasha.)* Cheer up, you two! We've come through the forest safely. I'm sure the people of this village will share their dinner with us.

SASHA: I hope so. My stomach is empty. It feels like a cave! *(Chief Forester knocks at Olga's door.)*

OLGA: *(Calling out of her window.)* Who is it?

CHIEF FORESTER: Only three foresters, walking home across Russia. Can you share some food?

OLGA: Food! No, I have nothing. Our harvest was bad. You will find nothing here. *(Turns from window.)*

PETYA: *(Knocking at Vera's door.)* Hello in there!

VERA: *(At window.)* What is it you want?

PETYA: Supper, if you have any. We are hungry foresters walking home across Russia.

VERA: I am sorry to see you so hungry, but you have come to the wrong shop. It is everyone for himself in these times! *(Turns away.)*

SASHA: *(Getting mad.)* Let's see if our luck is better here. *(Knocks at Dmitri's door.)*

DMITRI: *(Angrily.)* Who are you, anyway? Smart men are inside their houses, working.

SASHA: We are three foresters, sir. It would be kind of you to share your dinner with us.

DMITRI: I have just enough dinner for myself. If I share, I eat one quarter of a dinner and you get a quarter *(Pointing.)* and so do you and you. We shall all be hungry later. What good will that be? No, I do not believe in sharing. It's a very bad idea. *(Turns away.)*

PETYA: What selfish people these are!

SASHA: *(Loudly.)* They do not know how to share!

CHIEF FORESTER: Let's teach them a lesson!

PETYA: No, no! We won't rob anyone.

CHIEF FORESTER: Of course not, Petya. All I meant was to teach these people to make Stone Soup.

SASHA: *(Catching on.)* Ah, Stone Soup!

PETYA: *(Laughing.)* That's just the thing!

Scene Two

The Chief Forester and his companions are in a circle with their heads together, whispering. Dmitri is at the window.

DMITRI: Are you still here? Why aren't you on your way?

CHIEF FORESTER: *(Pretending not to hear.)* Get some wood, Sasha! Get the kettle ready, Petya. We will build our fire here, on this spot. *(Sasha goes off left. Petya finds two Y-shaped sticks on the ground.)*

PETYA: We can use these to hang the kettle on. *(Sets sticks in place.)*

CHIEF FORESTER: Perfect. Now for the stones. We must see if they have tasty stones here. Go and find some in that stream. *(Petya takes kettle to right. He throws some stones loudly into it. Olga and Vera turn and watch him from their windows. Sasha enters with dead branch.)* Good! That will heat our soup quickly.

SASHA: *(Lays fire, pretends to light it.)* What kind of stones will we use for our soup today?

CHIEF FORESTER: What kind do you want?

SASHA: Oh, something filling! Granite is a good stone. I always like a granite soup. It has body. It sticks to your ribs! *(Petya brings kettle to centre, rattling stones. Dmitri, Vera, and Olga leave houses, come near fire. Marya enters, followed by other Villagers.)*

DMITRI: *(Tugging Chief Forester's coat.)* Pardon me.

CHIEF FORESTER: Eh? Oh, it is you, my friend.

DMITRI: What did you say you are cooking here?

CHIEF FORESTER: *(In an offhand way.)* Just a stone soup. *(In a friendly way.)* Tell me, what kind of stone do you like? You might help us choose.

DMITRI: I! Why, I never heard of making soup from stones!

SASHA: You never heard of Stone Soup?

PETYA: I don't believe it.

CHIEF FORESTER: *(To Dmitri.)* Come, Sir. If you are not joking, you must eat with us. *(Petya shakes kettle.)* Have you some good stones there, Petya? Let Sasha choose.

SASHA: *(Examining stones.)* Hm-m! This chunky one—it will be good! Washed down from the mountain, it has a flavor of snow on it. Ugh! Throw that one away. A flat stone has a flat taste.

PETYA: How about the red one?

CHIEF FORESTER: No, no, that is only an old fireplace brick. It will taste like smoke. Nothing but fresh stones. We shall have a guest.

SASHA: Fill the kettle, Petya. My fire is ready. *(Petya dips water from well into kettle, hangs kettle over fire.)*

CHIEF FORESTER: *(To Dmitri.)* Have you a spoon? We foresters often make do with a stick. But for a guest, the soup will need proper stirring and tasting.

DMITRI: I have just the thing. It has a nice long handle. It is like new. I have not had guests in five years.

CHIEF FORESTER: *(Clapping him on back.)* Good work, you generous man! *(Dmitri goes inside for spoon.)*

SASHA: *(Smelling the air.)* Oh, it makes me hungry!

DMITRI: *(Returning with spoon.)* Here you are. Please be careful.

CHIEF FORESTER: Sir, you shall be served first. *(Stirs, tastes.)*

OLGA: Is it good?

PETYA: Good!

DMITRI: Good? *(Reaches for spoon.)*

SASHA: *(Keeping spoon away from him.)* Oh, so good!

CHIEF FORESTER: It might stand an onion, though. Onion is very good for pulling the flavor from a stone.

OLGA: You know, I might find an onion in my house.

FIRST VILLAGER: Hurry then, Olga. Get some. *(Olga exits.)*

SASHA: *(Tasting.)* Does it need just a touch of carrot? *(Villagers look at each other.)*

VERA: Perhaps I could bring some carrots for this soup.

CHIEF FORESTER: That is kind of you. And will you bring a bowl for yourself as well? You must eat with us. *(Vera goes inside as Olga returns with onions.)*

OLGA: Use what you like. I should like to learn to make this soup. *(Chief Forester adds onions, tastes. Petya tastes also.)*

PETYA: Should we add just a bit of potato, perhaps? I cannot say that Stone Soup is ever quite right without a potato or two.

OLGA: That is true. A stone is nothing without a potato! *(Vera returns with carrots and bowl. Chief Forester adds carrots.)*

MARYA: *(To Villagers)* Vera was invited, did you hear? How can we be invited as well? *(They whisper together. Marya calls out.)* If you need some potatoes for that soup of yours, I have a sack in my house! *(Marya appears with sack and gives the sack to Chief Forester.)*

CHIEF FORESTER: Many thanks. Please stay for dinner. And now, Sasha, let's get to business! *(Tasting.)* Add a

potato . . . another . . . another. *(Sasha is already ahead of Chief Forester's count.)* No, stop, Sasha. Stop!

DMITRI: What is the matter?

CHIEF FORESTER: Too many potatoes! The potatoes have soaked up the flavor of the stones.

VILLAGERS: Oh, too bad! What a shame!

MARYA: Is there nothing we can do?

PETYA: I have an idea. Meat and potatoes go well together. Let's add some meat.

DMITRI: I have a ham that will do the job. Wait here. *(Goes inside.)*

CHIEF FORESTER: It might work at that. *(Dmitri returns with ham.)*

SECOND VILLAGER: Good for you, Dmitri!

FIRST VILLAGER: Quick thinking!

ALL: *(Clapping.)* Hurrah, hurrah! *(Chief Forester adds ham.)*

MARYA: Can anyone make this Stone Soup?

PETYA: Oh yes. All you need are stones, fire, water—and hungry people.

CHIEF FORESTER: *(Tasting.)* Hm. Some stones, as you may know, contain salt. These from your brook do not seem to be that kind. *(Olga goes inside.)*

OLGA: *(Returning.)* Here is your salt. *(Chief Forester adds salt, with a big wave of his hand.)*

CHIEF FORESTER: Friends! Your attention, please! I know this will be a very good soup. You have fine stones in this village. Stay and eat with us, one and all. *(Villagers cheer and move about. First Villager goes offstage. She returns at once with bowls. Chief Forester fills them and all taste soup.)*

DMITRI: This is truly a delicious soup, folks! It has a good flavor!

MARYA: It fills you up!

DMITRI: And to think, neighbors, it's made only of stones! *(Foresters now move to stage front. They hold out their bowls of soup.)*

CHIEF FORESTER: *(To audience.)* Yes, think of that! It's made only of stones!

 Curtain.

The Little Rooster's Diamond Penny

by Marina McDougall
Illustrated by Kim LaFave

Long ago there lived a poor woman who had a little rooster. He wasn't just an ordinary rooster, although his mistress did not know it. They both lived in an old tumbledown cottage by the roadside.

One day as the little rooster was pecking away in the yard, he found a shining diamond penny.

"What good luck," the little rooster thought. "Now my mistress can go and buy some food."

At that very moment, the Sultan came riding by with his army. His eyes filled with greed at the sight of the diamond penny.

"Guards," ordered the Sultan, "take the diamond penny from this rooster at once!"

The poor little rooster scratched the guards with his claws and pecked their hands with his beak, but they were too strong for him. They took the penny from him.

The little rooster was very angry. Instead of running away, he flew up and hid inside one of the guards' cloaks.

Holding on very tightly, he managed to ride along with the guard all the way to the Sultan's palace. As soon as they arrived there, he sneaked out, flew to the top of the wall of the palace gardens, and started to crow.

"Cock-a-doodle-doo, Sultan, give me back my diamond penny!"

The Sultan stomped into his palace and banged the window shut. But the little rooster perched on the window ledge and made a louder racket than before.

"Cock-a-doodle-doo, Sultan, give me back my diamond penny!"

This made the Sultan very angry. He wasn't used to anyone going against his wishes.

"Go!" he said to his servant. "Catch that rooster and drown him in the well!"

The servant caught the little rooster by the wings and threw him into the well. But as soon as the little rooster hit the water, he did a very strange thing. He began to murmur to himself very softly.

"Gizzard, gizzard, magic gizzard, suck in all this water!"

And sure enough, soon all the water was gone from the well.

Then the little rooster shook the water from his wings, flew up to the Sultan's window, and started to crow again.

"Cock-a-doodle-doo, Sultan, give me back my diamond penny!"

The Sultan stamped his big foot and his face turned purple with rage.

"Go!" he shouted to his servant. "Catch that rooster and roast him alive in the oven!"

This time the little rooster didn't put up a fight. He even smiled a little to himself as the big servant threw him into the flames. As soon as the oven door closed on him, he started his magical chant.

"Gizzard, gizzard, magic gizzard, let out all the water and put out the fire!"

In an instant, all the water came spurting from his bottomless gizzard and soon the fire was out.

Very pleased with himself, the little rooster flew out of the oven through the chimney. Once again he perched on the Sultan's window sill and crowed at the top of his lungs.

"Cock-a-doodle-doo, Sultan, give me back my diamond penny!"

The Sultan's next command to his servant was even more cruel.

"Go!" he yelled. "Catch that rooster and throw him in the beehive. The bees will sting him to death."

The obedient servant snatched the little rooster by his tail and flung him into the beehive. When the servant left, the little rooster began his secret chant.

"Gizzard, gizzard, magic gizzard, suck in all the bees!"

As before, the bees quickly disappeared down the little rooster's throat.

Delighted with his trick, the little rooster clattered up to the Sultan's window and began to crow and clamor.

"Cock-a-doodle-doo, Sultan, give me back my diamond penny!"

In his fury the Sultan tore at his black beard. Then a slow, wicked smile spread over his face.

"Go!" he ordered his servant. "Catch that little rooster and bring him back to me. I'll handle him myself. I'll put him inside my bloomers and sit on him."

The little rooster could hardly wait to get into those big bloomers. As soon as he was inside the Sultan's pants, he murmured to himself.

"Gizzard, gizzard, magic gizzard, let out all the bees to sting the Sultan's seat!"

"Ouch, ow, oh my seat!" cried the Sultan, jumping up and down. "Take that little rooster to my treasure house and let him have his penny back!"

The guards escorted the little rooster to the treasure house and waited for him to pick out his diamond penny. Quick as a wink, the little rooster spoke the magic words.

"Gizzard, gizzard, magic gizzard, suck in all this treasure!"

In the treasure house there were three tubs full of money and seven chests of precious stones. When his gizzard was filled with treasures, the little rooster turned towards home and half flew, half ran until he landed at his mistress's front door.

"Look what I've brought you!" he cried loudly. He let out all the treasures from his magic gizzard right in front of the house. The sparkling mound of riches was as high as a mountain beside the poor woman's house.

The little rooster and his mistress danced with joy around the treasure heap, for they knew they would never again go hungry.

BOOK IT!

by Nicki Scrimger
Photographed by Brian Willer

There. You finished your story and sent it off to a publisher. If you're lucky, the company will publish your story. Here's how that happens and who makes it happen.

Getting the type and the art

You and your editor work together to decide on any revisions that will improve the story. Then you write the **final manuscript**, and the editor discusses it with a designer.

The designer's job is to plan what the book will look like with type and illustrations. First the designer works with the editor to agree on the size of type and the **typeface**. Here are samples of different typefaces.

This is a sample of 14 point Bookman.

This is a sample of 12 point Helvetica.

This is a sample of 10 point Rockwell.

Size of type is measured in points not millimetres.

Either the designer or the editor **marks up** the final edited manuscript. These marks tell the typesetter the typeface to use, the size of type, the width of the lines of type, and the amount of space between lines.

The typesetter sets the words of the marked-up manuscript in type. The long sheets of printed type are called **galleyproofs**. The editor reads these "galleys" and sends them back to the typesetter to correct any mistakes.

The designer cuts up the galleys and pastes chunks of text on cardboard **layout sheets**, leaving space for illustrations. This is a **rough paste-up** of what the book will look like.

The artist makes pencil sketches that fit the space on the layout sheets and that illustrate the designer's ideas. The editor and designer check this **rough art** and mark any changes that they want the artist to make.

Now you know where "proofread" comes from.

The computer terminal at the publisher's is connected to the typesetter's computer.

Putting the type and art together

The artist then prepares the color illustrations—**final art**—which the editor and the designer check very carefully.

Reproduction proofs of corrected type arrive from the typesetter. "Repros" are high-quality proofs so that the type will look sharp and clear when it's printed.

The designer pastes the **repro type** and photocopies of the final art on new layout sheets, using the rough paste-up as a model. These **final artboards** show exactly how each page of the book will look.

Blue lines printed on layout sheets help to make sure that the type and art are straight.

The scanner reads the art one color at a time.

Then the final artboards and the illustrations go off for filming—that's right, film! The **film negatives** of a book are like the negatives of photographs, only bigger. Here's how the films are made and used.

A printer needs only four colors of ink to print a book in full color: yellow, magenta (red), cyan (blue), and black. These four colors can make all the other colors.

The color separator separates the colors of each illustration into yellow, magenta, cyan, and black, using a scanning machine or a camera that takes special photographs. Each negative shows only one color, so for each illustration there are four films.

The repro type on the artboards is photographed separately. Then the films of the illustrations and the type are stripped together.

*So many checkpoints—
final manuscript, galleyproofs,
rough paste-up, repro proofs,
final artboards, film proofs,
press proofs.*

The editor and the designer check the film proofs for clear type and good color match with the artist's illustrations. After they OK the proofs, the films are sent to the platemaker.

The platemaker makes metal **plates** from the films. Plates made from the negatives for yellow will print only yellow, plates from the negatives for magenta will print only magenta, and so on. Each plate usually prints eight or sixteen pages, so there are four plates for each set of pages, one for each color.

Printing the book—at last!

If you visit a printer when a set of pages is being printed, you will see a stack of large blank sheets of paper at one end of a printing press and a stack of printed sheets at the other end. Here's what happens in between.

The four plates are wrapped around four cylinders on the printing press. The first plate has yellow ink, the second magenta, the third cyan, and the fourth black. As the sheets move through the press, each plate prints its color on the white paper. Where one color prints over another color, different colors are printed—magenta over yellow prints orange, cyan over yellow prints green, cyan over orange prints brown, and so on.

Press proofs are checked to correct colors that may be too dark or too light. Then the printer runs sheets for all the pages in the book through the press—printing first one side, then the other.

The last job is binding the printed sheets into a book. Machines fold the printed sheets so that the pages are in the right order. Then they gather the sets of pages and sew them together, trim the outside edges, and glue them into the cover of the book.

Now comes the final proof— will readers like your book?

Touch the Sky

- from *Who Hides in the Park*, illustrated by Warabé Aska

The Sack of Diamonds

by Helen Olson
Illustrated by Tina Holdcroft

One day many years ago—
so long ago in fact that
the sky did not have stars as it
does now— a little old woman, who
lived alone except for her dog, had her
one hundredth birthday.

The townspeople rejoiced with her and there was much feasting and dancing in the streets. Then, to the surprise of everyone, the king himself appeared and gave the little old woman a sack of diamonds for her birthday.

"Oh, me! Oh, my!" said the little old woman. "What a rare gift, a sack of diamonds!"

"Yes, indeed," exclaimed the people. "What a rare and valuable gift!"

Then the sun began to set and, after bidding the others good-bye, the little old woman hurried home with her sack of diamonds and her dog. She did not want to be out late as, unless the moon was out, the starless nights were very dark indeed.

The next morning the little old woman sat in her little chair in her little house and considered what to do with the sack of diamonds.

"It is a rare gift, indeed," she said to her dog. "But I already have everything I need. I have my little house, my garden, and my warm cloak which will last for many a year."

Suddenly she jumped up from her chair. "Here I am sitting," she said, "when I should be up and about hiding this valuable treasure so it will be safe from robbers."

No sooner had she said this than she dug a hole in her garden and buried the sack of diamonds. But the dog immediately dug them up and brought them back to the little old woman.

"Oh, me! Oh, my!" said the little old woman. "This will never do."

Next she hid them in the well. But when she took a drink of water, she had to spit it out because it tasted of the sack.

"Oh, me! Oh, my!" said the little old woman. "I will hide the sack of diamonds in the chimney!"

However, when she started a fire, all the smoke came into the house because the diamonds had stopped up the chimney.

"I cannot stand this," said the little old woman. "I will have to think of something else."

She strapped the sack on her back. But her back ached so much from the weight that she soon had to take the sack off.

"Oh, me! Oh, my!" she said. "What to do? What to do?" And so saying, she sat on the sack of diamonds, but it was so uncomfortable that she soon had to get up.

"I wish I were rid of these diamonds," she said to her dog. "They have caused me nothing but trouble."

Early the next morning the little old woman loaded the sack into her wheelbarrow. She pushed the wheelbarrow to the town square, and there she left her burdensome treasure.

Then she returned home with the empty wheelbarrow.

"Oh, me! Oh, my!" she told the dog. "How glad I am to be rid of those diamonds!"

Just then there was a knock on the door. Some townspeople were standing on the doorstep. They set down the sack of diamonds.

"We have found the sack of diamonds the king gave you,"
they said. "It was in the town square."

"Imagine that!" said the little old woman.

After the townspeople had left, the little old woman
shook her head.

"Oh, me! Oh, my!" she said. Then she opened the sack
and looked at the diamonds. They sparkled and sparkled.
"The diamonds are pretty," she said to the dog, "but they
are of no use to me."

Then she sat down in her chair, put her chin in her
hand, and thought and thought.

Suddenly she jumped up. "Oh, me! Oh, my!" she said,
"Now I know what to do. Why didn't I think of it sooner?"

She set to work immediately. Soon she had finished
making a fine, strong slingshot.

That night she went outside with the sack of diamonds and the slingshot. It was pitch black outside, as it was most nights.

Then with her slingshot the woman shot one diamond after another into the sky. There the diamonds stayed, making the night sky bright.

By the time she had gotten rid of the whole sack of diamonds, the sky was filled with twinkling lights, where they still twinkle away to this very day.

The little old woman was well pleased with herself.

"Now the diamonds are of use to everyone," she said to her dog. "And now I can enjoy my old age in peace without that sack of diamonds cluttering up my house!"

Star Light, Star Bright

by Monica Kulling

What makes a star bright?

The Seven Sisters of the Pleiades

A star is like a huge burning ball, and its fire gives off the light we see. The fuel for its fire comes from different types of gas. When these gases come together, they burn—and they give off heat and light. These gases provide the fuel for the life of the star.

Is the Sun a star?

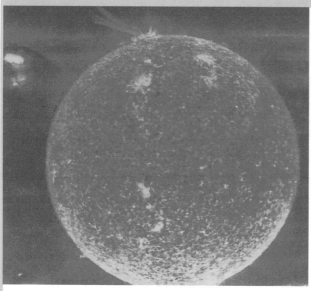

Apollo telescope shows solar eruption

Yes, the Sun is a star—a huge ball of burning gases. It gives off heat and light to Earth. The reason it looks bigger and brighter than the other stars is that it is much closer to us on Earth. If the Sun were as far away as the other stars in the sky, it would look as small as them.

Why do stars disappear in the daytime?

The stars are always in the sky, even during the day. But we cannot see them because the light from the Sun is too bright. The stars "come out" at night when the Sun is setting and the sky begins to darken. The darker the sky gets, the more stars we see. There are billions of stars in the Milky Way Galaxy.

Trail of Echo satellite against the Milky Way

Andromeda Galaxy, the nearest large spiral galaxy

Just a small part of the Milky Way, showing veil nebula in Cygnus

What is a galaxy?

A galaxy is a group of stars and planets, of gases and dust, all held together by gravity. (Gravity is the force that keeps us from falling off the Earth.) There are billions of stars in each galaxy, and there are many galaxies in the Universe. But the Milky Way Galaxy is our galaxy.

What is the Milky Way?

When you look up at the night sky, you can see a hazy band of light stretching across the sky. The stars in this hazy band are only part of the Milky Way Galaxy. There are billions more that you can't see. These stars and the Sun and the nine planets, including Earth, that spin around it are all part of the Milky Way Galaxy.

Is the Sun the hottest star?

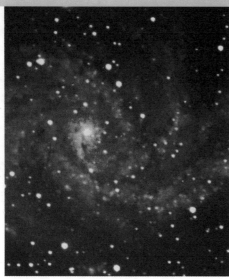

No, there are many stars that are hotter than the Sun. The hottest stars are bluish in color, just like the centre of a candle flame. The coolest stars are reddish in color. The stars that have a relatively medium temperature— neither the hottest nor the coolest—are yellow in color, like our Sun.

A spiral galaxy, with hot blue stars

Are stars all the same size?

Stars come in different sizes. The Sun is a medium-sized star. It is bigger than all the nine planets in our Solar System put together. So, as you can imagine, it's pretty big! But there are stars that are many, many times bigger than the Sun. Betelgeuse, in the constellation of Orion, is 400 times bigger than the Sun. A star called Epsilon Aurigae is 5,000 times bigger than our Sun.

The constellation Orion, the hunter

What is a constellation?

Look up into a clear night sky and you will see some bright stars that form a pattern or "star-picture." If you could connect the stars like a dot-to-dot puzzle, you might see the outline of a hunter, a great bear, or a queen. People with a lot of imagination first named these star-pictures, or constellations, many years ago.

And we still use the names today:
Orion—the hunter,
Ursa Major—the great bear,
Cassiopeia—the queen.
But the constellations change position with the seasons, so it's hard at first to recognize their patterns. A good guide book helps—one that shows the imaginary star-to-star outline of each constellation.

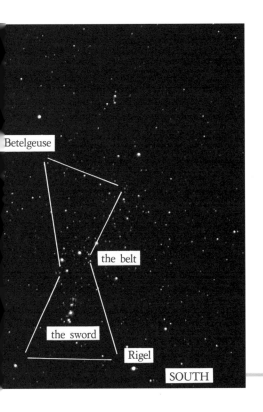

Artist's interpretation of the Greek hunter

The Paper Crane

Written and illustrated by Molly Bang

A man once owned a restaurant on a busy road. He loved to cook good food and he loved to serve it. He worked from morning until night, and he was happy.

But a new highway was built close by. Travellers drove straight from one place to another and no longer stopped at the restaurant. Many days went by when no guests came at all. The man became very poor and had nothing to do but dust and polish his empty plates and tables.

One evening a stranger came into the restaurant. His clothes were old and worn, but he had an unusual, gentle manner.

Though he said he had no money to pay for food, the owner invited him to sit down. He cooked the best meal he could make and served him like a king.

When the stranger had finished, he said to his host, "I cannot pay you with money, but I would like to thank you in my own way."

He picked up a paper napkin from the table and folded it into the shape of a crane. "You have only to clap your hands," he said, "and this bird will come to life and dance for you. Take it, and enjoy it while it is with you."

With these words the stranger left.

It happened just as the stranger had said. The owner had only to clap his hands and the paper crane became a living bird, flew down to the floor, and danced.

Soon word of the dancing crane spread, and people came from far and near to see the magic bird perform.

The owner was happy again, for his restaurant was always full of guests.

He cooked and served and had company from morning until night.

The weeks passed.

And the months.

One evening a man came into the restaurant. His clothes were old and worn, but he had an unusual, gentle manner. The owner knew him at once and was overjoyed.

The stranger, however, said nothing. He took a flute from his pocket, raised it to his lips, and began to play.

The crane flew down from its place on the shelf and danced as it had never danced before.

The stranger finished playing, lowered the flute from his lips, and returned it to his pocket. He climbed on the back of the crane, and they flew out of the door and away.

The restaurant still stands by the side of the road, and guests still come to eat the good food and hear the story of the gentle stranger and the magic crane made from a paper napkin. But neither the stranger nor the dancing crane has ever been seen again.

Birds on the Wing

by Susan Hughes

When you jump into the air, you can stay up for only a few seconds. Then gravity pulls you back to the earth. But birds can stay in the air for hours, or even days! What do they have that we don't have?

Birds are built for flying. They have bones and feathers that make them very lightweight. Most bones of birds are hollow with thin walls. They act like airpockets inside the bird. Also, birds are mostly feathers, and feathers weigh practically nothing!

Birds also have wings to help them fly. But not all wings are the same, and not all birds fly in the same way. Some birds soar, some birds flap their wings quickly. Some birds hover, some birds dive, and some birds cannot fly at all! Look at a bird's wings and you can tell a lot about how, or if, the bird will fly.

The long, pointed wings of a gull or the broad wings of an eagle are made for soaring. Wind and rising currents of air push up against the broad surface of the bird's wing. The bird can glide slowly downward through the rising air without moving its wings.

The wings of a pigeon or duck are general-purpose wings. They are made for flying from place to place, not for soaring.

Can you see the hummingbird's tiny wings? It beats them so quickly they look like a blur! The hummingbird can hover in one place while it sips nectar from a flower. It can even fly backwards!

The loon spends most of its time in the water, not in the air. The loon can fold its wings tightly against its body when it dives, smoothly and quickly, under the water. It doesn't have hollow bones, and this makes it a great diver, but not a very good flier. The loon must flap its narrow wings long and hard before it can lift its heavy body out of the water and into the air!

Some birds, such as penguins, have wings but do not fly. The penguin's narrow wings are like flippers. It uses them to move very quickly through the water. Penguins also use their wings for balance as they walk or hop from rock to rock.

Many birds are capable of long-distance flight. Look up to the sky in the spring or autumn, and you may see birds migrating. The greater snow goose flies from the Arctic to the southern United States or Mexico every autumn. Thousands of these geese stop for a rest in Cap Tourmente, Quebec, during their long journey.

Birds are soaring, diving, gliding. Birds are swooping, flapping, hovering. Birds are on the wing!

The Most Beautiful Kite in the World

by Andrea Spalding
Illustrated by Suzanna Denti

Jenny ran quickly down the road toward the school. If she ran fast, she had one whole minute to spend inside the General Store. One whole minute to look at the most beautiful kite in the world.

"Excuse me, how much is the big red kite?" she asked the storekeeper.

"Five dollars and ninety-five cents," he answered.

Jenny frowned. She had only seventy-five cents in her piggy bank, but tomorrow was her birthday. Maybe her father would buy her the red kite as a present.

The school bell rang, and she skipped carefully down the sidewalk avoiding all the cracks and humming to herself. *"Step on a crack, break your back. Take a hike, fly a kite."*

That night, as she fell asleep with all her fingers and toes crossed, she dreamed of a kite that trailed sunbeams and flew her to strange, far-off places full of balloons and butterflies, heaving seas and pirate ships.

Her birthday dawned, golden and gusty.

"*Perfect kite weather!*" she thought and jumped out of bed, hurriedly dressed, and ran into the kitchen.

There was a kite-shaped parcel by her breakfast bowl. Jenny ripped off the wrapping paper in long strips.

It was a kite. But not the big red one from the store, not the kite of her dream. This was a home-made one. She recognized the light wood from her father's workshed. He must have worked while she was asleep, shaping the frame and covering it with white paper.

Her throat felt tight and dry.

Her father came into the kitchen whistling. "Good morning, Jenny. I see you've found your present. Like it?"

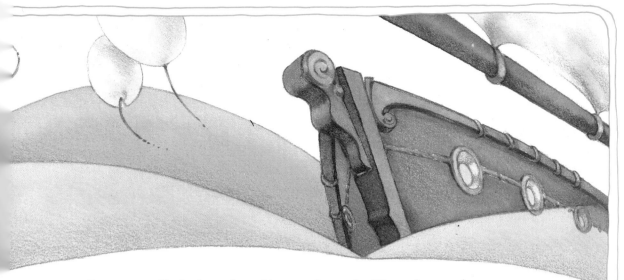

Jenny smiled, but her lips quivered. Her throat hurt too much to speak, but she ran over and gave him a big, hard hug.

"Eat your breakfast," he said happily, "and we'll go out and see how your kite flies."

The food stuck in Jenny's throat. She only nodded.

They walked out into the spring sunshine. Her father had a bounce in his step, but Jenny's feet felt like lead, and her eyes watered.

"It's the dust," she explained.

Her father took a roll of string from his pocket and helped Jenny attach it to her kite.

"I'll hold the kite while you let out the string," he instructed. "Then, when I shout, run into the wind."

Jenny waited while he carried the kite several paces away and held it up to the breeze.

"Ready, Jenny? Run!"

Jenny ran. But the kite only swooped and dragged in the prairie grass. She sighed with disappointment.

"Hmm," said her father, "that's what I need to know. It's nose heavy, needs a tail." He tied a loose piece of string to the bottom of the kite. "Look around, Jenny. See if you can find anything to make bows for the tail."

Jenny scuffed her shoes in the dirt. "*Why should the kite need bows and a tail?*" she thought. "*The red kite would have flown perfectly the first time.*"

On a nearby porch sat their neighbor, Mrs. Omelchuk. She was knitting a yellow sweater and enjoying the early morning sunshine. Jenny walked slowly over.

"Please could you spare me some wool? I need to tie bows on the tail of my kite."

Mrs. Omelchuk gave her a big yellow handful. Jenny took it to her father and stood back to watch him tie three bows that gleamed like sunbeams.

"*That will never work,*" she thought disgustedly.

"Come on, Jenny. Let's try again." Her father held the kite high above his head. "Are you ready with the string? Run!"

This time Jenny felt the string lift as she sped into the wind, and she glanced back hopefully. But a moment later the kite fell to the prairie. It was still nose heavy. Jenny stamped her foot.

"I knew it wouldn't work. This kite will never fly," she cried in frustration.

Her father came over and placed his arm around her shoulders. "Sure it will," he reassured her. "We just need more bows to balance it."

"Really? That's all it needs?" asked Jenny. She looked thoughtfully at the kite. It *had* flown better the second time, and the wool from Mrs. Omelchuk did look pretty.

Her father smiled and ruffled her hair. "Yup, that's all. Just two or three more bows . . ."

"And WHOooOOSH, up it goes!" Jenny laughed. And she ran off to find them.

Mr. Braun was reading a magazine with a bright red cover. Jenny bounced up to him and cleared her throat. He grinned at her.

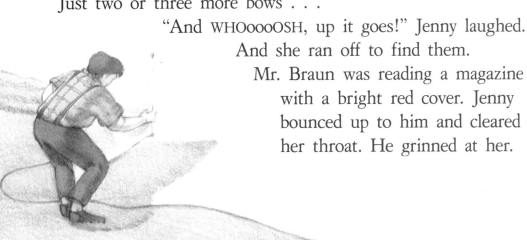

"Excuse me, but I'm trying to get my kite to fly."

"You need help, *liebchen?*"

"We need bows for the tail, and I thought . . ." Jenny hesitated. "Do you need the cover for your magazine?" She blushed.

"I flew kites when I was little. They were fun." Mr. Braun gave her the red cover.

"Oh, thank you, thank you!" Jenny ran to her father waving the cover triumphantly. "Dad, let's try this."

Carefully tearing the paper, they knelt together and added two more bows to the tail. Once more, her father held the kite up.

"Ready, Jenny?"

Jenny nodded eagerly and turned into the wind. She ran swifter and surer than before. The kite quivered and rose for a minute. Then the wind dropped, and it fell, smack, to the ground.

"Oh, rats!"

Her father pretended he had not heard. He picked up the kite and balanced it thoughtfully. "One more bow should do it."

Jenny looked around. A movement caught her eye. Leaning against a truck, her friend Charlie was peeling a purple wrapper from an all-day sucker.

"Hey Charlie," she yelled. "Trade you a fly of my kite for that paper off your sucker."

"Doesn't fly yet." Charlie stuck the sucker in his mouth.

"It will if we tie another bow on the tail."

"Well . . . I guess so." Charlie passed Jenny the wrapper, sauntered over, and watched.

Jenny tied the purple bow to the tail, handed the kite to her father, and eagerly held the string. Once more he lifted the kite to the breeze.

"One, two, three . . . Now!"

Jenny ran. Her feet sped lightly over the grass.

Slowly and uncertainly, the kite rose, dipped, then caught the air current and soared upward. Jenny turned, feeling the string come alive.

"Quick! Let out more string," called her father.

She carefully unreeled. The kite pulled and climbed and responded. Jenny's face filled with an enormous grin.

There above her, soaring, dipping, and playing tag with a meadowlark, was a magical sight. The early morning brightness caught the kite, held it, and turned it to dazzling gold. It was Jenny's dream kite! A sunbeam golden kite that swept the sky with a tail of bobbing yellow, red, and purple butterflies.

Around her gathered her father and Charlie, then Mrs. Omelchuk and Mr. Braun. They all looked up in wonder.

"Ooh," they said, "how beautiful."

"Yes," beamed Jenny. "It's the most beautiful kite in the world," and she floated across the prairie with her feet barely touching the earth.

The next day, Jenny ran quickly down the road, past the General Store, to the school. If she ran fast, she had one whole minute before the bell rang. One whole minute to show her friends the most beautiful kite in the world.

Birds on a String

Illustrated by Helen D'souza

To a Red Kite

by Lilian Moore

Fling
yourself
upon the sky.

Take the string
you need.
Ride high,

high
above the park.
Tug and buck
and lark
with the wind.

Touch a cloud,
red kite.
Follow the wild geese
in their flight.

The Kite

by Helen Ball

If
my heart
were only a paper kite
I'd toss it high in the morning light
and let it fly, the giddy thing
till it touched the sky
then, bye and bye
I'd cut
the
s
t
r
i
n
g

Up, Up, and Away

Have you ever wished you could float up into the sky in a balloon? It looks so easy, but getting a huge hot-air balloon up in the air is a tricky job. A team of experienced people must fill an empty nylon bag with hot air without having it lift off before it should.

First, the balloon has to be carefully unpacked and laid flat. Then it has to be inflated two-thirds full of cold air. That's done by using a large fan. One person aims the fan while two or three hold open the throat of the balloon.

Next, a couple of the team members walk inside the balloon to check the seams for leaks. Once that's been done, they attach the basket. Some baskets hold one person, others are big enough for five or six.

Now comes the tricky part. The team makes one final safety check. Then the pilot turns on a powerful propane burner on top of the basket. When everyone is ready, he lights a "sparker." Fire shoots into the balloon.

The balloon is laid flat.

It is partly filled with cold air.

Fire shoots from the "sparker" into the balloon.

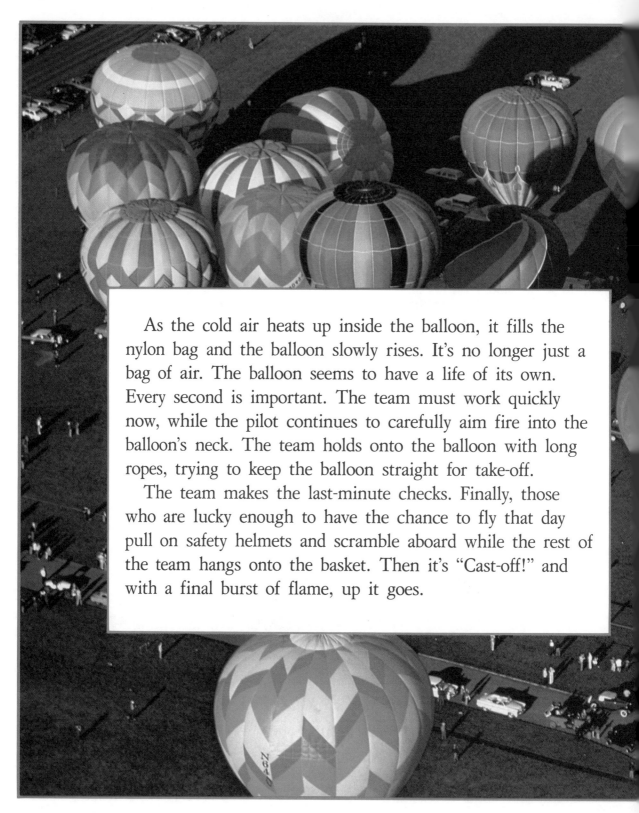

As the cold air heats up inside the balloon, it fills the nylon bag and the balloon slowly rises. It's no longer just a bag of air. The balloon seems to have a life of its own. Every second is important. The team must work quickly now, while the pilot continues to carefully aim fire into the balloon's neck. The team holds onto the balloon with long ropes, trying to keep the balloon straight for take-off.

The team makes the last-minute checks. Finally, those who are lucky enough to have the chance to fly that day pull on safety helmets and scramble aboard while the rest of the team hangs onto the basket. Then it's "Cast-off!" and with a final burst of flame, up it goes.

The cold air heats up; the balloon begins to rise.

Up, up, and away!

Hot-Air Henry

by Mary Calhoun
Illustrated by Erick Ingraham

Henry wanted to fly. Everybody in his family had gone up with the balloon, but The Man always declared, "I'm not flying with that cat!"

The Man had been taking pilot's lessons, and this time he was going to solo. Henry grumbled and his tail switched as he watched the people crunch around on the crusty March snow.

The Kid and The Woman held open the mouth of the colorful balloon, while The Man blew it up with a gasoline-powered fan.

Then the Instructor blasted warm air into the balloon from the burner mounted on a frame below it.

"Watch your fuel gauge," he told The Man. "You don't want those propane tanks to run dry. And stay away from those power lines on Colson Hill."

At last the beautiful balloon stood fat in the air. The Woman and The Instructor loaded the fan into the truck. The Kid held down the basket while The Man jumped out to get his camera, which he'd forgotten.

Henry saw his chance to stow away. He raced across the snow and leaped up to the basket. One of his claws snagged on the cord that fired the burner, and there was a horrible roar.

"Grab that cat!" yelled The Man.

The Kid lunged for Henry and slipped on the snow.

The burner kept roaring. Flames heated the air, and up rose the balloon.

Up rose Henry, up, up, and away! Henry was flying!

He shook his claw loose from the cord, and the burner stopped roaring, but the balloon kept on lifting.

Henry crouched on the leather rim of the basket, digging in his claws.

Below, the ground fell away, and the people shouted and waved. Yet the basket didn't feel as if it were moving, and Henry wasn't afraid.

"Yow-meowl!" he called down to The Kid. He was Hot-Air Henry, the flying cat!

The balloon surged up the sky. Looking down, Henry saw the river like a black ribbon winding between white fields. The Kid and The Man looked small as cats. The balloon drifted silent as a cloud, and Henry loved the glorious bubble that carried him across the sky.

Balanced against a post on the rim of the basket, Henry floated above his snowy world. To a tune of The Kid's about "Sailing, sailing, over the bounding main," Henry sang, "Yow-me Ow-me Ow-meow-meow." He was the cat to sail the skies!

But now he'd had his flight, and it was The Man's turn to solo. Time to go down. How?

Henry stood up and tried pulling the cord. The whooshing roar of the burner scared him, and he tottered on the edge of the basket. To keep from falling, he clung to the cord, and the burner kept roaring, and the balloon rose higher.

That was not the way to get down out of the sky.

Henry hopped to the basket floor and searched for something to push or pull that meant Down. Nothing.

Standing on his hind legs, he peered over the edge of the basket. He couldn't see his people anymore. And the balloon was sailing toward the mountains. Where was Colson Hill with those power lines?

Henry glared up into the bright cave of the balloon. "Come down now!" he yowled.

Then he saw a cord leading down from the balloon. He could reach it from the rim of the basket. When he clawed the cord, he saw a little hole of sky open in the balloon cloth. As air spilled out, the balloon began to sink.

Faster and faster, the basket dropped, toward the ground—too fast!

Henry let go of the cord. More slowly the basket sank toward the river, black rushing water—a splash-down?

No, the basket crunched on the snowy bank. "Ha!" breathed Henry.

But the basket bounced up in the air again, touch and bounce, over the snow.

"Stop it!" Henry yelled at the balloon. "I'm not a yo-yo!"

Ahead were some willows dotted with blackbirds singing, "O-kal-lee!" The basket bounded over the tops of the trees, brushing out birds.

"Tchk, tchk!" The redwings swarmed around the basket. Henry snatched at this bird, that bird. Missed! Missed!

The birds whisked upward, teasing, "O-kal-lee, you can't catch me!"

Henry forgot about landing. "I can too!" he yowled. Standing on the rim, he pulled the burner cord.

Roar, the basket zoomed after the birds. "Yow-meow!" Henry chased blackbirds up the sky.

But the balloon overshot the birds, and they settled back down in the willows. The balloon sailed on toward the mountains. The wrong direction, away from The Man and The Kid.

"Go back!" yowled Henry at the beautiful bubble. But the balloon went where the wind took it.

Below, a lazy eagle coasted on an air current flowing in the right direction. Maybe if the balloon dropped just to that level—

Henry crept around the rim of the basket and pulled the air-spilling cord. Slowly the balloon sank and began to come around. It didn't take off after the eagle like the tail of a kite, but it was going more toward The Kid than away.

"Yow-meow-ee!" Henry sang out. He'd show that balloon who was boss! He, Hot-Air Henry, would bring the balloon right back where it started from.

He toed his way along the rim and pulled the burner cord just a flick to keep the balloon from dropping too low too soon.

At the roar of the burner, the eagle flapped up in surprise. "What in the sky!" screeched the eagle. The big bird circled the fat contraption. Henry watched anxiously. That eagle better not peck a hole in his balloon!

"Snaa!" Henry hissed. "Scat! Get away from there!" He made the burner roar.

"Help!" squalled the eagle. "What a cat, to roar like

that!" The eagle winged away from the fearsome feline.

Henry spared a paw to smooth his whiskers. Then he peered down, narrowing his blue eyes at the brightness of the snow. Below on a road was a truck, and The Kid's head stuck out the window. The chase truck was following the balloon.

"Yow-yow, right now!" sang Henry. He got over to the rip cord, spilled air, and the balloon dropped.

Just then, "Honk, honk," came a squadron of geese flying straight at him. "Honk," called the geese, "honk, honk!" What did they mean, *honk*? He would *not* get out of the way!

The V of geese broke up around the balloon, and they rushed up and down, squawking. But the head goose sat down on the edge of the basket by the burner cord.

"Snaaa!" hissed Henry. "Get out of my basket! You can't perch there!"

"Honk! I can too," said the head goose, perching there.

The balloon kept sinking.

"Hey, Cat!" The Kid's shout made Henry look. The basket was headed for some high-strung power lines. At last he'd found Colson Hill. He had to fire the burner to lift quickly, or he'd sizzle on the wires. But the goose guarded the burner cord.

Henry started toward the goose, "Snaaa!"

"Hiss!" answered the goose, hunching its wings.

Henry had never fought a goose, and he didn't like to try for the first time while balancing like a tightrope walker.

But he had to fire the burner!

Henry sprang. Over the goose's head he leaped, onto the goose's back, and clawed at the cord. As Henry flew over, a sharp nip of a beak on his tail made him yowl.

But when the burner boomed, the goose jumped into the
air. And Henry fell off its back—into the basket, which
soared up over the power lines. Henry licked his throbbing
tail, while the geese re-grouped and flew on. "Honk, honk."

Then Henry pulled the rip cord to bring the basket
down. The Kid and The Man jumped out of the truck.
The basket bounced once over the snow toward them, as
Henry hung on to the air-spilling cord.

The Man grabbed the dragline, then the basket.

"Mew." Henry drooped against a post. The Man might be
mad at him for going off with the balloon.

Henry leaned his head on The Man's chest. "Purr-mew!"
he begged pardon for soloing sooner than The Man.

"Wow, some high-flying cat!" said The Kid, punching
down balloon cloth.

"Purr-mew!" said Henry, smoothing The Man's chest.
Wise old flying cat.

EMMA'S FLIGHT RECORD

Nine-year-old takes off in bid for flight record

Emma Houlston, a 9-year-old who first learned to fly while sitting on her father's knee, has taken off on a journey she hopes will make her the youngest person to pilot a plane across Canada.

Emma, of Medicine Hat, Alta., wrapped up the first leg of the flight from Victoria yesterday when she landed her father's Grumman AA-5 in Kelowna, B.C.

She left Victoria on July 10 and hopes to reach Newfoundland in two weeks.

"I've only been flying for a few months but I think I can do it, and Dad will be with me anyway," said Emma, a Grade 3 student who is too young to hold a pilot's licence.

Paul Houlston, a licensed flight instructor and vice principal of his daughter's school, is going along on the trip as the legal "pilot in command." He said Emma will handle routine flying, the navigation, and the radio, but she does not have the experience to handle an emergency.

A video camera mounted in the cockpit will monitor the flight to ensure that he does not fly unless there is an emergency.

Houlston started teaching Emma to fly eight months ago after he had heard about Christopher Marshall, who flew across the United States last year at age 10.

"I began to wonder if Emma would be able to handle such a trip," Houlston said. "About four weeks ago when we finished her training, I realized she could, so here we go."

"I'm quite excited," Emma said before takeoff.

Crossing Rockies 'bumpy' for pilot, 9

Emma Houlston crossed the Rocky Mountains and, after a short while of bouncing around the clouds, made a smooth landing in her home town of Medicine Hat yesterday. About 25 residents, including her classmates, came out to greet her.

"It was all right, but a bit bumpy," Emma said of her passage over the Rockies. Her father said Emma was able to maintain good speed because of a strong tailwind over the mountains, although she got airsick because of the turbulence. But she did not let go of the controls, he added.

The pair originally planned to fly non-stop from Kelowna, B.C., to Medicine Hat, but put down for the night in Cranbrook because of thunderstorm warnings issued for the Crowsnest Pass region.

After resting most of the day and overnight here, Emma was to get behind the controls again this morning and take off for Regina. She hoped to land in the Saskatchewan capital at about noon.

FLYING START: **Emma Houlston, 9, has a run on the tarmac at Victoria's airport yesterday. The Alberta girl hopes to become the youngest person to fly across Canada.**

Flight across Canada is a lark for 9-year-old

WINNIPEG, MAN. (CP)

Emma Houlston says she is not flying a light plane across Canada only for the recognition—it is also a great vacation.

"I don't care if I get in the record books or not, it's the flight I want to make," she said after landing in the Manitoba capital yesterday.

Emma said the flight is less tiring than the hoopla. "I got up at 5:45 this morning for an interview," she said. The toughest part of the trip was over the Rocky Mountains. "It was really windy and bumpy over there."

Her father, Paul, agreed. But over the Prairies, he said, the problem is "the stress and boredom you get from looking out at those limitless horizons."

Emma is gaining valuable experience, her dad said. "She is improving and I'm really impressed with her."

"I act as the co-pilot and do some of the navigation, but none of the actual flying. I don't touch any of the primary controls."

Emma said she has never considered quitting. "I know that I can make it," she said, twirling her long straight hair with one hand, while clutching a stuffed dog in the other.

She enjoyed landing in the expansive city of Winnipeg on the fourth day of her trip. "It was nice; it's huge compared to Medicine Hat," she said with a giggle.

Canadian Press

177

Pilot, 9, lands in Sudbury as heavy fog blankets Wawa

By Jane Armstrong
Toronto Star

SUDBURY, ONT.

Undaunted by heavy fog, Emma Houlston caught a strong tailwind yesterday and sailed past Wawa to land safely in Sudbury.

She is now about midway through her attempt to become the youngest person ever to fly a plane across Canada.

"Wawa was fogged in so we couldn't land there," said Paul Houlston. He said they were aiming for Wawa when they left Thunder Bay about noon.

"We dodged over to (nearby) Chapleau, but we were at 2900 m and sailing along on a 30- to 40-knot tail wind so we decided to just keep going to Sudbury," he told Canadian Press shortly after the two touched down in Sudbury at about 3:15 p.m.

The unscheduled detour shaved a full day off her schedule, and the junior flying ace hopes to reach Ottawa sometime today.

Yesterday's heavy fog was Emma's second bout with inclement weather in three days. On Friday, the father-daughter team was grounded in Winnipeg because Thunder Bay was fogged in.

Earlier, Paul Houlston said Emma's biggest problem is that she gets bored just sitting still and looking at the scenery. Houlston bought some tapes of children's books to occupy her.

Her father said that the average of three hours of flying a day should not be too taxing for Emma, who is doing all the actual piloting, including landing and taking off.

"I just sit there and navigate and Emma sits and tries to keep the plane on the straight-and-narrow," said her father.

"I used to think she was just a kid, and she is. But I hadn't realized just how grown up she is."

The Toronto Star

Sudbury

178

Pilot Emma, 9, still on course in bid to set Canadian record

OTTAWA, ONT. (CP)

Emma Houlston was all smiles as she stepped onto the tarmac at Rockcliffe Airport just before 1 p.m. yesterday. She and her father arrived 30 min ahead of schedule on their flight from Sudbury.

They were lucky with the weather and had a trouble-free flight. They were to stay at the Chateau Laurier Hotel, but they had time to visit the Parliament Buildings before settling in for the night.

Emma and her father were to leave Ottawa early today for Montreal, then Fredericton, N.B., Charlottetown, P.E.I., and Sydney, N.S. They have about ten days to go in their journey to St. John's, Nfld.

Canadian Press

My flight plan:

Canadian Press

Emma finishes record flight across Canada

ST. JOHN'S, Nfld. (CP)
Nine-year-old Emma Houlston became the youngest person to pilot a plane across Canada when she landed here yesterday after a five-hour flight from Sydney, N.S.

Clutching her stuffed mascot, the Alberta schoolgirl brushed off reporters' questions about the trip. But she admitted that she did not think she would try it again.

"I don't know," she said. "Once is enough."

The leg to Newfoundland was considered the trickiest of the flight. Most of it was over open water in air corridors noted for unpredictable and unfavorable winds. Houlston said his daughter had no trouble with the flight. "I could hardly believe our luck when the weather was reported as good for the entire trip."

I Did it!

COUNTDOWN TO TAKEOFF

from OWL *Magazine*

You're booked on a 10:00 a.m. flight from Toronto to Vancouver. It will take at least 100 people to get your flight off the ground. Here's a look at what some of those people do.

11:30 p.m., Sunday: 10 1/2 hours to go

While you're snug and warm in bed, a team of cooks is working all night long. They're preparing the food for your flight, including special meals for passengers on unusual diets. By the time you're awake, all the meals will be arranged on individual trays and packed into huge containers, ready to be loaded on the plane.

Midnight, Sunday: 10 hours to go

The aircraft you'll be flying in landed at Toronto a short while ago. As soon as the last passenger disembarked, the cleaning crew swung into action. In just over an hour, the inside of the jumbo will be spotlessly clean. Fortunately, jumbos rarely get dirty on the outside—they fly above most pollution. But if a scrub-down is needed, long-handled mops and soap and water do the job.

2:00 a.m., Monday: 8 hours to go

After the cleaning crew finish, ground mechanics go to work on the plane. They're doing a "layover check" and it's carried out every time an aircraft is on the ground for more than six hours. By the time you're ready to drive to the airport, every part of the plane will have been checked.

A fuel truck pulls up to the aircraft and a fuel technician jumps out. It takes 20 min or more for the truck to pump up enough kerosene jet fuel from the airport's underground supply to fill all the jumbo's tanks. If your car could run on jet fuel, there would be enough in a DC-10's tanks to drive it around the earth 21 times!

8:30 a.m., Monday: 1 1/2 hours to go

While you were eating breakfast, an operations control agent was working out how to balance the load—fuel, passengers, cargo, mail and food—so that the plane flies level. Now the ramp crew is loading cargo and mail containers into the hold.

9:00 a.m., Monday: 1 hour to go

As you're arriving at the airport, the captain is studying a computer-prepared flight plan. The computer is given information about the weather, wind direction, weight of cargo, and where the plane is going. It then comes up with the best fuel-saving route possible. Once the captain has the flight plan, he and the flight crew board the plane and begin a careful check of all the aircraft's instruments and systems.

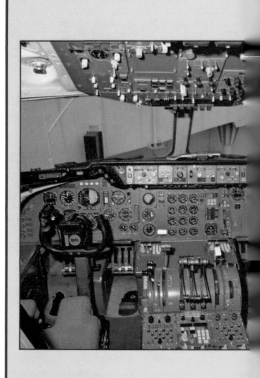

9:15 a.m., Monday: 45 minutes to go

At the check-in counter a passenger agent enters your name into a computer, which assigns you a seat. As you're passing through security on your way to the departure lounge, the second officer is walking around the exterior of the plane making a final safety check. And your luggage? It's gliding into the basement of the terminal on a

conveyor belt. There it's loaded into a container and by the time you're seated on the plane, your luggage will be in the hold.

9:45 a.m., Monday: 15 minutes to go

Inside the cabin the "No Smoking" and seatbelt signs come on. While the cabin crew is demonstrating safety equipment to you, the captain is receiving clearance from the control tower to leave the loading bridge. As unlikely as it might seem, a little tractor will push your jumbo backwards until it can manoeuvre on its own.

10:00 a.m., Monday: Takeoff

After final clearance from the control tower, your plane quickly accelerates down the runway, and at about 300 km/h it's up, up, and away.

Spaceman from Another World

by Lee Harding
Illustrated by Harvey Chan

An alien starship was circling Earth to observe life on the planet. Tyro, one of the aliens, was making repairs on the outside of the starship's hull. He was working inside a huge robot-like spacesuit, and he was manipulating the controls to make the repairs.

But the alien engineers forgot about the repairs—and about Tyro! They fired up the spaceship's engines and took off for home, sending poor Tyro tumbling—still inside the spacesuit— over and over toward Earth.

Erik and Stephen saw the spaceman fall. They were playing by the creek when it happened.

At first they heard a far-off, high-pitched whine. It sounded like some sort of aircraft, only different from anything they had ever heard. In a moment it had grown into a desperate rushing sound that made them look up.

The sky seemed to split open. The noise grew into a frightful roar.

from The Fallen Spaceman

186

They saw something small and dark and smoking streak down from the sky. It crashed into the forest, not far away from where they stood.

The strange object was not stopped by the treetops. They could hear it tearing a way down through the trees. A second later the ground shook beneath their feet. Birds flew screaming into the sky and the whole forest was in an uproar.

Gradually the air grew still again, and Erik looked at his younger brother. "Now what on Earth was *that*?" he said.

Stephen shrugged and looked uneasy. He was only seven and there were many things he didn't understand. He rubbed his nose and stared at the trees, a little scared by what they had seen.

"Could have been a meteorite," Erik said, thoughtfully. "One of those falling stars."

"What if it's a UFO?" Stephen said.

An unidentified flying object? Erik nodded. Well, why not? You read enough about them—maybe they *did* exist. Some people called them flying saucers. Neither of them had ever seen a UFO, but they *might* exist. It was rather like ghosts, Erik thought—you had to see one before you were convinced.

The falling object had been smoking, so it must have burned up in the atmosphere. Maybe it was only a meteorite, after all.

"Come on," he said, urging his little brother to join him. "Let's go have a look at it. . . ."

Erik set off at a run. Stephen was slow to follow. He was uneasy about stepping into the forest, and doubtful of what they might find there. He didn't share his older brother's interest in outer space . . . but he didn't like being left alone, either.

"Wait for me, Erik," he called out. And ran after him.

But they did not run for long. The slope of the field grew steep. Their pace had slowed to a walk well before they reached the edge of the forest.

It was dark and gloomy among the tightly packed trees.

"Why don't we go back and get Dad?" Stephen wanted to know.

"Don't be a scaredy," Erik said. "I bet it's only a small meteorite, that's all." He took his brother's hand and stepped cautiously into the forest.

Erik sniffed the air. It was heavy with the smell of

scorched earth. The object must have been very hot when it reached the ground. Stephen pressed close against his brother. "I wish Dad was here," he kept saying. But Dad was some distance away, back with Mom at their summer house.

Ahead they could see where the falling object had torn a great cleft in the trees. Erik hurried forward, dragging his little brother behind. They squeezed through some dense ferns and then . . .

They stood on the edge of the wide clearing newly carved from the forest. At the centre of the clearing a huge blackened object lay crumpled on the ground. It looked like a giant made of metal, stranded on the floor of the forest and burned black.

"*What is it?*" Stephen whispered.

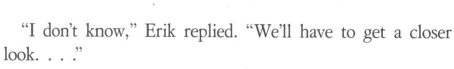

"I don't know," Erik replied. "We'll have to get a closer look. . . ."

Stephen pulled back into the shadows. "You go, Erik," he said. "I'll wait here."

As Erik drew closer he saw that the object was shaped roughly like a man—twenty metres tall!

Erik could make out enormous arms and legs and a strange, ugly head. The huge legs ended in great treads, like a tractor, and each one was the size of a car.

If this thing was truly a spacesuit, he thought, then it must belong to a creature so big that it could only have come from another world!

Another world . . .

"Erik," Stephen called out from the edge of the ragged clearing. "I want to go home now. I want to tell Dad." He looked forlorn and frightened, hunched down in the undergrowth. He didn't want to get any closer to the fallen spaceman.

Erik waved him to be quiet. "In a minute," he called back. "I just want to get a little closer. . . ."

He waited a moment, but the giant gave no sign that it could move.

What if the . . . the creature inside had been killed by the fall? Erik wondered. Or what if he was only unconscious?

He frowned and looked up at the great cleft torn through the forest. It seemed unlikely that anyone could have survived such a dreadful fall. And yet . . . *and yet . . .*

He crept cautiously around the great helmeted head.

He wasn't surprised to find a faceplate on the other side. It was mostly covered with dirt and twigs where the head had plowed into the ground.

He took a deep breath and leaned forward, scraping some of the dirt away with nervous fingers. The glass was still warm but not so hot it could not be touched.

When most of the dirt had been removed, he bent closer and peered through the glass.

It took a few moments for his eyes to adjust. The faceplate was dark, like sunglasses, but after a while he thought he saw something moving inside. . . .

Complete illustrations from which details were used in unit openers

Illustration from *Annabel Lee,* by Edgar Allan Poe; illustrations copyright ©1987 by Gilles Thibault. Reprinted by permission of the publisher, Tundra Books.

Illustration from Pete Seeger's Storysong *Abiyoyo;* illustrations copyright ©1986 by Michael Hays. Reprinted by permission of the publisher, Macmillan Publishing Company.

Illustration from *Who Hides in the Park.* by Warabé Aska; copyright © 1986 by Warabé Aska. Reprinted by permission of the publisher, Tundra Books.